MICHELLE G.
MELISSA LASON

# PANDEMONIUM,

# ARIZONA

JOURNALSTONE
YOUR LINK TO ARTIST TALENT

ISBN: 978-1-68510-049-0 (sc)
ISBN: 978-1-68510-050-6 (ebook)

First printing edition: May 27, 2022
Printed by JournalStone Publishing in the United States of America.
Edited by Sean Leonard
Cover Design by Don Noble
Proofreading, Cover Layout and Interior Layout: Scarlett R. Algee

JournalStone Publishing
3205 Sassafras Trail
Carbondale, Illinois 62901

JournalStone books may be ordered through booksellers or by contacting:
JournalStone | www.journalstone.com

This book is dedicated to my biggest supporters and my whole world,
Ricardo, Bobby, and Kiki.
—Michelle Garza

This is for my husband, Chris, and my little angel, Kahlan.
—Melissa Lason

We would also like to dedicate this to our horror family, such an
amazing group of fellow writes and readers. We appreciate you all
more than you will ever know. Also extra thanks to our horror sister,
Scarlett, for taking a chance on this gory, ridiculous book!
—SoS

Content Notes:

This book contains depictions of sex work, bodily functions, extreme
violence, and off-page abortion.
Please be advised.

# GUSANOS IN THE FIELD OF DEATH

PIECES OF WIRE stuck out of the earth, masked by the powdery desert dirt covering them. Hector knew what they were attached to and was careful not to step on them as he made his way towards the old barn. The smell hanging in the air was putrid, one he was certain would remain with him even after a bath. It was a stench he often found stuck in his nostrils after leaving his boss's property, but he still never got used to it. His stomach lurched into his throat. He put his hand over his mouth and stood still, calling upon all of his willpower to hold the vomit in. He swallowed it back down into his broiling gut. He didn't want to leave any pieces of himself behind on the cursed ground of the field of death, not with the three working inside of the barn. They didn't hide their distaste for him, and the things they could do with even a drop of his bile made his skin crawl.

\*\*\*

The three were flown in all the way from Catemaco, a Mexican city built on black magic. *Los Tres Gusanos*. In the tongue of the gringo, their names roughly translated to "the three worms"—specifically maggots, which was very fitting to their nature. They were paid by Hector's boss to enact rituals of power and vengeance. Hector was raised Catholic but never questioned the morals of his boss, Chamuco, a man who chose a nickname of the devil as his alias. Hector only did as he was told and waited for his pay, as most did in the wastelands of Arizona.

\*\*\*

It was nearly dusk, a fact that weighed heavily on Hector's mind. He wanted to deliver the message and then get the hell away from the den of death before the watchful moon could rise. He was nearly to the door when it creeped open, sending chills up his spine. They already knew he was there. He slid the crucifix around his neck down into his shirt before proceeding.

"*ENTRA!*"

Hector nearly lost his stomach again, only this time it threatened to empty out the other end at the command of the leader of the three, El Gusano. His voice was not completely human, deep and gurgling like a toad. Hector stepped into the barn; he always tried to mentally prepare himself for the sight of the inside of the barn of death, but it never helped. The dirt floor was sticky with blood in thick pools, stains even the dark didn't conceal. There were wooden tables holding bowls of brains and other random organs. An altar was erected at the opposite end; Hector never ventured close enough to fully inspect it. Instead, he always remained within feet of the door. He didn't speak as he held out an envelope to the ghastly man who stood shirtless, tattoos running up his arms. Gusano's bloated stomach appeared unnaturally large hanging over his thin legs. Like his namesake, he was hairless, his scalp covered in scabs. With long, twisted fingers the *brujo* took the letter, then passed it to his sisters who sat around a splintered table poking at a putrid corpse with a long strip of wire fastened to its neck. Hector averted his gaze, not wishing to look into the milky eyes of the dead man they had yanked from the soil like a fish pulled from a sea of cursed sand.

The twins were short and stocky, their greasy hair braided down their backs. They smiled toothless grins at the messenger, knowing they frightened him, as they peeled black strips of meat from the corpse. The only distinguishing difference between them was one sister had a series of warts rimming her lips. Hector shuddered, his hand fidgeting at the collar of his shirt, desperately seeking the comfort of his crucifix. He'd handed out death warrants before, and knew the fields surrounding the rickety barn were filled with dead bodies, but seeing one so horribly decomposed nearly cracked the thin veil of composure Hector managed to muster. He desperately held his nausea at bay as his mouth filled with saliva and a cold sweat glistened on his forehead. El Gusano laughed at Hector, a rattling phlegmy guffaw. He turned to his sisters and they giggled, too, as the one with a marred mouth opened the envelope. She nodded and her brother came to her side and when she whispered into his ear, he looked to Hector intently. The other twin spoke her mind, knowing the contents of the letter through the connection she shared telepathically with her sister.

"*Los gallos?*" she huffed. "*Puta madre!*"

Hector knew she was unhappy trying to sway the outcome of cockfights, for she was a woman of power and deemed it below her. Her dingy cotton dress clung to her rear end as she waddled from the table to a crowded shelf and rummaged through an assortment of jars and dried herbs until she found what she sought. Hector anxiously waited for the *bruja* to return with two cloth bags, one black and one red. She gripped his outstretched hand in hers, hesitating, watching him squirm under her gaze. Her fingers felt like worms against his skin, knotting his stomach in disgust as she placed the small bags firmly in his palm and whispered his instructions.

\*\*\*

When he was free of the barn, Hector took off running for his car without any shame. Once inside, he pulled the crucifix from his shirt and kissed it. The skin of his chest burned. He ran his finger over a cross-shaped blister before starting his engine and speeding back to the main highway. His heart thudded the whole dark drive until the lights of Apache Wells lit the horizon. His breathing evened out and he eased his foot from the gas pedal. He needed to sprinkle the contents of the red sack onto his boss's prized fighting rooster; the black was to be poured over Cuervo's rooster before the match in order to assure Chamuco's victory. Behind him, he could see two headlights in his rearview mirror, two big yellow eyes following him. Hector recognized them; he always felt uneasy when he caught a glimpse of them speeding up at his back. He guessed there were more instructions in the letter he was sent to deliver, perhaps a job he was unaware of. *Los Tres Gusanos* were on their way to complete Chamuco's most secret orders, and someone was going to die. Hector crossed himself and prayed his name never ended up in an envelope given to the *brujo* and the twins. They were frightening enough when they were on the same team, but to become their enemy...he'd rather swallow broken glass.

# IRRITABLE BOWEL SYNDROME

THE CAB OF the truck rocked and in the driver's side window hung a pair of neon-green thong panties.

"Carla, that fuckin' cow," Wanda muttered to herself, and continued her search for an empty truck.

Carla was the new bitch, a thieving little whore who wore the most obnoxious-colored clothes and underwear. She had taken Wanda's shift on the late nights, which meant Wanda was stuck working mostly evenings, which made her cash flow dwindle. She snuck over at night on occasions to nab a few customers, but if her boss caught her she'd have hell to pay...and a few times she did. Wanda knew by the rig it was Larry who was sharing the new prostitute's company and it made her laugh out loud. He was known to enjoy strange sex practices, and she wouldn't be surprised to find Carla in the truck-stop ladies' room cleaning a steamer off her chest when it was over.

The thought of the ladies' room made her gut lurch and she hot-footed it in that direction. She often wondered if she didn't have irritable bowel syndrome. She had seen a late-night infomercial about it once and it seemed to describe her erratic shitting habits perfectly. Her ankle rolled painfully in her haste and she stumbled against the graffiti-decorated door. A loud-mouthed junkie named Ritchie hovered around the perimeter of the stinking restroom, but he didn't halt Wanda like he did other folks because he knew her pimp's level of crazy far exceeded his own. Instead, he took one look at her and strutted away, leaving her to her business. Night had fallen and insects swarmed the yellow light above her, arriving quickly to inspect the perspiration brought on by the sudden urge to crap.

"Fuck!"

Her stomach bottomed out, and the need to take a shit came with such ferocity she worried it would soon be running down the legs of her flesh-colored pantyhose. She pulled the heavy steel door open, hurried inside, and shoved it closed. It was now an intricate dance, holding her ass cheeks together, slipping and sliding on the constantly damp floor, and jiggling the door until the lock slid into place. She kicked her feet free of her silver pumps and yanked off her white fake-fur coat. It was a single-stall restroom and its solitary commode was decorated by the hundreds of women who chose to hover above its seat. She wiggled and pulled her denim skirt up above her waist with one hand while the other feverishly tore the pantyhose down. She knew then, as she shook and sweated her cheap makeup into a clown-like display of beauty, that choosing a plate of chili fries for lunch was a horrible decision. It came out in a hot explosion, a volcanic eruption of feces, leaving the toilet to appear as though someone had loaded a double-barrel shotgun with runny poop-shot and blasted it a few times, peppering it with fecal matter. The first wave abated, but her anus kept spasming and leaking liquefied turd. It didn't exit with much force, instead dripping out and sliding down her legs. The last of the toilet paper was about three sheets of piss-soaked one-ply, so Wanda knew she'd have to hit up the sink. She scooted along with her legs bound up in her pantyhose and stood before the mirror—just a sheet of polished steel due to the countless times it had been shattered—and that's when she realized the terrible mistake she had made, which explained the awkward trajectory of her shit spattering everywhere. She'd forgotten to pull down her thong.

"Motherfucker!" she said to her reflection.

Taking hobo baths in sinks wasn't a new concept to her, and neither was washing shit from her thighs, but the whole situation required far too much time. If she didn't hurry, Jim might catch her as she exited the restroom and he'd surely send her on her way, more than likely with a black eye. Wanda slid her thong down and instantly regretted buying underwear two sizes too small as they rolled up and got stuck on her thighs, wringing out brown liquid down her calves and onto her feet. She basically had to wash her entire lower half in a small hand sink with little to no water pressure and a hand-soap pump that had run dry months before.

She left the restroom feeling five pounds lighter and mostly clean from the waist down. She left her thong and pantyhose in the trash can and hurried to return to work. Nervous fear shot through her at the sight of her pimp, Jim Dandy, waiting for her. He was a true albino and looked as harmless as a little white mouse, but he was an evil bastard right down to his soul.

"Where'd you come from? Goddamnit!"

"I just came down to see if there was any work tonight, any open trucks?"

He balled his fists but didn't swing. He spat a wad of chewing tobacco on the ground and thought for a second, then said, "Cherry got picked up by some pigs down by the liquor store, so I guess you can stay, but you know my take is higher since you disobeyed my orders."

Relief flooded Wanda, loosening her twisted stomach knot. He had a meticulous way of scheduling work for his "employees." Most of the time it made no sense to Wanda, but she knew what could happen if she went against his commands. It was all psychological, a way for him to assert his control over the poor women of the night, but there were very few places she could ply her trade in relative safety so she abided by Jim's power trips.

"Tiny needs some company!" he said, eyeing her.

She nodded, her hand straying to her stomach.

"What's your damn problem?"

"I had an emergency," she said.

She knew it was useless to try to explain her bowel problems. Jim was an asshole and didn't accept excuses.

"Get over there, he's waiting!"

She made her way quickly across the gravel parking lot in the dark, thankful to earn a few extra dollars.

\*\*\*

Tiny stood outside of his rig and wrung his hat in his hands like a shy child.

"Sorry, Tiny. I was feeling sick to my stomach."

"That's okay, Wanda Sue. Maybe tonight you can just put it in yer mouth if your stomach hurts."

She smiled; he was a thoughtful man. "All right."

The cab of his truck smelled like sweat and onions, his usual body odor. She grimaced, but from the looks of the parking lot he might be her only john for the night and she knew she could get through it. He climbed in behind her and started clearing space in his sleeper for her to sit. He had to push aside his collection of *Beaver in the Bush* magazines and empty takeout containers. It wasn't anything new to her, all the clutter and junk; she had learned it was the clean ones she had to watch out for. The meticulously tidy ones usually ended up asking to choke her or have her stomp on their nuts or some crazy shit, so when she climbed into a pigsty like Tiny's she knew she would probably be safe and able to get out of the situation with the usual penetration of her twat, mouth, or rear end, all three if they were willing to pay enough.

"How's your night?" he asked as he unzipped his jeans.

Wanda hated making small talk with her clients, but she didn't want to upset Tiny. He had always been kind to her and she didn't want her attitude to force him into the arms of another lot lizard like Carla, the chatty little bitch.

"It's been long and kinda shitty, but it's almost done."

"I'm sorry you've had a hard day," he said.

"Comes with the territory."

"I heard this territory also has a problem with drug gangs and what-not, you ever see anything like that around here?" he asked.

Wanda shook her head. "Nope."

She was lying. She had watched shady business go down, even dabbled in a little nose candy herself, but had kicked it to the curb when she found herself hooking day and night to get it. She wanted to ask Tiny if he worked for the fucking DEA, but kept it to herself for fear of running off a good customer.

"I saw the patrol cars all along the side of the highway a couple days ago. I think they must have found a dead body or something..."

In truth, Wanda couldn't count how many people had gone missing or turned up dead in the last six months. The death toll was rising in Apache Wells, and it made her nervous to leave her trailer at night, but she had bills to pay. She also knew that even though Jim was an abusive prick, he wouldn't let anyone seriously hurt or kill one of his ladies as that would put a dent in his cash flow. She had watched with her own tired eyes the lines of mysterious cars and trucks blazing down the highway, but she had also heard whispers of a sheriff who looked the other way while holding his hand out for a kickback. She knew better than to play private detective or continue in any conversations alluding to crooked business with johns.

"There's lots of dead bodies, honey, all over the United States. I know you didn't come to see little old me to talk about dead bodies, so let's talk about something else. What do you want?" She tried to make her voice sound erotic, but she could hear the exhaustion in it and winced.

"I think you know," he said.

She ran her hand up his thigh, and he blushed. The polite talk and gossiping about the body parts found along the highway was done.

He pulled down his pants and the stench grew with such intensity she could already taste him on her tongue. He shed his underwear to reveal his genitals; his prick matched the rest of him, short and thick. His pubic hair was out of control and she had to spread it apart to maneuver her mouth over him. As always, he sighed and his thighs shook. Her eyes fell upon a bulbous boil just above his knee; it had a head on it and was constantly filled with yellow pus. There were others she knew of on his chest and back. They were ALWAYS there. It repulsed her, but she always found herself fighting the urge to smash the shit out of them and finally get rid of the damn things. She felt sorry for Tiny; it seemed God had truly shit on him when it came to the looks department, but how many unattractive afflictions could a single soul be cursed with? He was extremely hairy, the stench of him spoke to his lack of hygiene, and he had hideous boils speckling his pasty flesh. She worked him rapidly, knowing he was lonesome and didn't get attention from women unless he paid for it. He shot off quickly, leaving her mouth filled with his bitter taste. He pulled his pants up over his ghost white thighs, hiding the pus-filled lump, and struggled to button them below his gut.

"Thank you, Wanda." He held out two twenty-dollar bills.

"It's only thirty." She spoke before realizing the words had come out.

"A little extra, maybe you can get you some ginger ale for your stomach." He was still breathing heavily and mopping sweat from his face on a handkerchief.

She felt a pang of shame for thinking badly of him; who the hell was she anyway? She was no longer young nor what most men would find attractive, especially after her nights on the lot. She smiled at Tiny and shoved the money down her bra.

"Thank you, Tiny."

# WHAT THE NIGHT BRINGS

TINY LEFT HER on the dark sidewalk at the edge of the truck stop. The highway was mostly empty coming into town, but there were a few big rigs barreling along in the night. It always made her feel a strange sense of loneliness to look out in the darkness. She could see miles of black desert, black highway, and *saguaros* like giant skeletal hands reaching to the sky. She imagined it a desolate, forgotten graveyard, one she'd never escape from. It was where many men like Tiny were left to their own devices, their own thoughts and deeds. The open highways were where they were free to be who they really were. Most people never got to see much more than a fake smile or a wave from a window from these men, but Wanda did. Some held kind, chivalrous qualities, like Tiny, while others had violent, psychotic sides. She was their fantasy woman, with a mouth like a sealed tomb that never opened to reveal its ghosts. She could never speak the truth as to what she saw in dark truck cabs by the distant light of a secretive moon. She tried once, in a roundabout way, to tell her neighbor Roy, but she was too drunk and rambled incoherently. She knew he would never understand.

A car sped by, its engine racing, and it didn't slow down until the yellow lights of the city washed over it. She had seen it before, running up and down the highway, always in a hurry wherever it went. Whoever piloted it must be a man of business, not the corporate type, but of drugs and blood. He was a person she didn't want to cross. Behind it crawled a beast of a car, a jet-black hearse going the speed limit as if the driver had no reason to hurry. She felt her skin crawl because she had seen it before, too, and it belonged to a monster. She thought of Tiny's tale of a possible body on the roadside and shivered; if anyone would leave a body to rot in the sun, it would be the man behind the wheel of the hearse. Wanda knew better than to speak her thoughts out loud. She was never unlucky enough to see the backseat of the hearse, but she guessed those who did wouldn't be there for a fuck or a suck, but to be driven off into oblivion, beyond the city lights, where only the coyotes bore witness to death's coming.

"Hey, get your flabby ass over here!" Jim's voice hailed her.

His quick strides told her he was finished with seeing her around the truck stop for the night, and though she needed money, she felt relieved. After watching the hearse drive by, she just wanted to go home to her trailer. The sight of that car reminded her of death, and brought her mind circling back like a vulture to a loss she could never let go of.

"Show me what you made, hand it over!" Jim demanded, and she obeyed.

\*\*\*

The church was dark. The candles had burned down and everyone had gone home, leaving it echoing with phantom voices of prayer. Padre Guillermo walked down the center of the great, old building; the rows of pews on either side of him grew silent and empty. He was heading toward the doors to lock up for the night. It was something he didn't used to do, in case any lost souls sought refuge, but after hearing a recent confession he didn't feel safe leaving them unlocked anymore.

Cuervo had made him a promise; the church would never be touched. The priest agreed to allow him to meet in secret there with other men of bad reputation, but those clandestine meetings were no longer a secret, and Padre Guillermo knew that would bring dire consequences.

He had almost reached the door when he heard the wind pick up outside, carrying the calls of coyotes. He looked to the window across the church, where the aged sycamore trees towered beyond the glass. They were absolutely still. He shuddered as the doors blew open. Padre Guillermo stood at the threshold of the door; sitting on the grand cement stairs leading to the church were three shadows. One was taller with thin legs, while the two on either side of it were short and broad. Amidst the utter darkness of the silhouettes glowed pairs of eyes, like predators beneath the moon. The unnatural wind died, and a voice spoke to him in a language he didn't understand, like Latin spoken backwards. His heart seized in his chest; the devil had come to Apache Wells, and it had hunted him down.

He turned to run, but the burning in his chest had stolen his breath. He couldn't move, he couldn't scream. He felt his knees buckling beneath him. His vision blurred as he fell sideways out the doorway. The impact ignited a hot explosion of pain in the side of his head. He tumbled over and over down the hard steps and landed at the feet of the three shadows.

# A MESSAGE SENT

DAVID WASN'T SENT with the *brujo* and his twin companions. As the hours passed, it made him wonder and worry a bit as to what job they were tasked with. He hadn't trusted the three since his boss brought them to the ranch; they gave him *malas vibras*. Over a short amount of time they had gained Chamuco's complete trust, and David blamed their spells and charms, they had bewitched his boss. He felt Chamuco pushing him aside and turning only to Gusano and the sisters for advice. David was becoming useless, a very dangerous state to occupy in their world. His feelings of apprehension towards Chamuco's plans couldn't be hidden, and David's outright defiance of them was growing too obvious. There were too many orders of senseless killings, too many grotesque requests, things he knew had nothing to do with the drug trade and had much to do with the three living out in the old barn. David wasn't a grave robber, he wasn't a man who scoured the desert for coyote bones and toads. It was all too much for him, shit was getting far too weird.

Chamuco had been quiet towards him most of the day, a sign there was trouble. David grew paranoid and his conscience told him he had fucked up. He should have kept his mouth shut, but he had lost himself in a bottle and swam back out only to make the biggest mistake of his life.

All he could remember was the church smelling of polished wood and candles, his heart overflowing with grief at the loss of who he considered more of a friend than a boss. Chamuco was no longer himself; he was controlled by the *brujo* and the twins. David's mind was crowded with knowing what was planned: a great war. He couldn't allow Chamuco's plans to be carried out, it was against the *codigos*. David's father taught him that there was a way their business should be carried out, and a way it shouldn't be. The old man came from the old school, he was a member of *la vieja guardia*, and he refused to allow his son to become one of the new *narcos* who only wielded blood and *plomo* before intelligence and negotiation. His father despised the new generation, said they were too flashy, too hot headed, didn't know how to operate from the shadows, which was unnecessarily dangerous. His father died of old age, an uncommon form of death in their trade, but even on his deathbed he warned his son of Chamuco and how he had a hunger for greed in him. He told David that Chamuco was becoming a monster. David took it to heart and never forgot. His boss was operating in a dishonorable way.

\*\*\*

David's footsteps sounded too loud on the wooden floor; he even glanced down and begged his boots to tread more quietly. He was there in secret and didn't want anyone to rat him out. He was technically walking in enemy territory, but how would Cuervo even know the pact was going to be broken unless David got the message to him? Cuervo was like his father in many ways: he wanted success, but he wanted it coupled with anonymity and as little death as possible.

Father Guillermo was busy walking among the pews, making certain no personal belongings were left behind as he always did, and didn't notice David's entrance.

"Padre," David said softly.

Padre Guillermo turned and looked on him with wary eyes; he, too, had heard rumors of Chamuco's growing penchant for violence.

"*Aqui es territorio neutral.*"

David felt ashamed that the priest was frightened by his presence. He knew Chamuco's name was growing as a man who dealt out death, but to scare a man of God with the face of one of his servants was sickening.

"*Si, yo se,*" David said, and pointed to the confessional booth. "*Estoy aqui para hacer una confecion.*"

Padre Guillermo looked at him suspiciously, his honey-colored eyes inspecting him down to his soul until David turned with his hands raised to show he wasn't armed.

"*Por favor, es importante.*"

\*\*\*

David went to his room and pulled open his top dresser drawer. There was a stack of cash and an extra clip for his gun. He took them both and grabbed the keys to his truck. He didn't need anything else to survive. He would drive nine hours into Mexico, and there, in Obregon, Sonora, he'd find protection with his cousin. He refused to wait and see if Chamuco would discover his treachery, and Cuervo wouldn't be able to shelter him if Chamuco's war ended in his favor.

He was gathering pictures of his father from the side-table next to his bed when all the hair on his arms stood up. His door opened and an elongated shadow spilled across the floor at his feet. He didn't have to turn around to know El Gusano had darkened his threshold. The *brujo's* shadow crawled up David's legs and its spindly fingers held him there. David refused to scream; he wouldn't grant the bastard the satisfaction. Gusano tossed something at his feet. David's breath caught in his throat when he recognized two honey-colored eyes. The priest was dead and David knew he talked. The deadly truth was uncovered. He silently asked God to make his death as swift and painless as possible, but as the thought passed his mind, the *brujo* laughed. He had read David's thoughts, and David knew he was in for complete torment.

"*Ratoncito, la verdad es como la caca, siempre flota a la superficie.*"

# CHAMUCO

HE STOOD IN the moonlight. His plans seemed to be coming together just as predicted. He would destroy the old crow Cuervo. Chamuco knelt in the desert sand and lifted his hands to the sky, the power of the night settling over him. He was but an amateur in the arts of black magic, nothing compared to *Los Tres Gusanos*, but they promised to lift him to the heights he deserved. He would become the supreme ruler of all the lands for as far as his eyes could see. When he located them on a trip to Catemaco, he was hoping to find the way to make his own shoddy use of black magic stronger. He felt an instant draw to the bald *brujo* and his twin companions. They were a horror to look upon, but he didn't shy away from them. He knew in his heart they were his ticket to power. His only hope in defeating Cuervo and his men, they would help Chamuco bring down the old empire and replace it with his own.

He felt the eyes of the *brujo* on him. He saw Gusano standing in the darkness of the barn door, smiling like a wolf in the night, his eyes glimmering with unearthly light. The *brujo* nodded his head and Chamuco plunged his hands into the powdery sand, and his fingers caught the end of a rusty wire. He pulled with all his strength until his palms were cut and bleeding, but he managed to free the wire from the earth and what came along with it struck a chord within him. The severed head of a local priest, a man Chamuco had sentenced to die only hours before. It had jagged holes cut through the flesh of its cheeks and wire strung through it. The head hung dirty and dripping dark blood from where it would have connected with its neck. The priest's eyes were missing, but Chamuco could never forget the face of the man who aided and abetted his rival for many years and granted him the sanctuary of a church to hold his secret meetings with other cartels from south of the border. Padre Guillermo had refused Chamuco's requests to hold his own meetings and his proposal to switch sides. The priest let his mouth run too much and he was silenced for it. Chamuco was very pleased. The Gusanos had already fulfilled his order, and soon it would be his turn to repay them. Their request had always been the same: They longed for Pandemonium, and Chamuco would grant it to them.

# THE WITCHBOARD

SHE HAD WONDERED so many times what had kept her hooking for twenty years. Becoming a lot lizard hadn't been a childhood dream, obviously, but when Wanda had started at seventeen, it was fast money and left her feeling empowered. Now, at thirty seven, she felt used up. She walked home to her trailer in the park behind the truck stop. Her fridge had the remainder of the eighteen pack of Busch she had bought the night before, and she planned on polishing it off. She didn't get to keep the extra money Tiny was kind enough to give her. Jim Dandy had taken it during his nightly "inspection." The stingy bastard checked all the ladies before he allowed them to go home, just in case they tried hiding extra tips. She'd learned years ago that it was easier to just to fork over all that she made. She was lucky to get to keep thirty percent of her meager earnings anymore, while Jim lived high on the hog. Carla, the little bitch, got to keep fifty percent most nights. It was quickly becoming clear the new bitch was Jim's favorite, and it irritated not only Wanda but his three other veteran ladies. And what were they supposed to do about it, form a union for hookers?

The trailer park was poorly lit and surprisingly quiet, but she figured since it was a Wednesday night most people were already asleep. Her feet ached and she knew there would be blisters left from the silver high heels she had purchased from the thrift store. Her stomach was empty and growling, but she didn't feel much like eating after the incident in the restroom. Her condition was always in the back of her mind, and tonight was a reminder of what happened when she made poor eating decisions. She was completely unaware of being watched from the shadows of a broken-down station wagon left to rust in her neighbor's side yard.

Wanda was standing at her front door, digging through her lavender-colored purse in a search for her keys, when the assault came fierce and suddenly. The backs of her legs felt as if they caught fire, her skin peeling away beneath the talons of her attacker. The quick puncture wounds dripped trickles of warm blood.

"Fuckin' rooster! Again!" Wanda screamed.

She turned to see it, standing knee-high to her, a massive rooster with blood-red feathers. Her neighbor's prized possession. It eyed her, its head twitching side to side. She knew it was ready to come at her again. She stepped backwards, her back pressed against her trailer door. It ruffled its feathers and launched itself like a crimson projectile, all claws and beak. She reacted the same way she treated any rough cocks, by swinging her overstuffed purse at it with all of her strength. The rooster was batted away and landed in the dead grass of her lawn, its head hanging from a limp neck, but still it ran in circles. It made such a raucous she worried its owner, Roy, might awaken. She kicked off her heels and fell upon it using one of the silver pumps to bludgeon the rooster from hell, its life clinging to it like a sticky turd, and she marveled at the beating it took to finally put it down. Its fighting name was Jean Claude Van Damme, at least that's what Roy called it, and Wanda now knew why. The damn thing was stronger than a coked-out martial artist, and had more life in it than the Terminator.

The night was silent, and she made her way quickly into her home with the rooster corpse shoved down into her big-ass lavender purse. She peeped out the window and was relieved to see her tussle with Jean Claude didn't wake any of her neighbors. She wrapped the dead rooster up in a Piggly Wiggly bag and shoved it in her trash can under the kitchen sink. She cracked open a beer and slammed it; it was refreshing and finally washed away the taste of Tiny from her tongue. Wanda belched loudly; even if she didn't live alone, she wouldn't have felt any shame from it. It was a bodily function, every human being in the world did it, just like pissing, shitting, sleeping, or fucking. And that was how she lived, shameless and content, most of the time.

Wanda went to her bathroom and showered in cold water—the water heater hadn't worked in months, but she never had the cash to replace it. She knew if she called her landlord, Gene, she would "owe" him, and last time that meant a month of licking his asshole. There were things she never liked to do, and tossing salads was at the top of her list. She stood before her mirror and studied her lanky body. Her breasts were never very big though they were still perky, but her ass was flat as a board. Her hair was yellow and wavy and needed a dye job, but Jim Dandy only paid for it every four months. Her face really showed the years of hard living: her teeth were stained and crowded, and the wrinkle lines around her eyes and mouth seemed to age her ten years. She chugged her beer and ran a brush through her hair. She was pulling on a pair of underwear when a drop of blood halted her.

"Shit!"

Wanda rummaged through her bathroom drawers and then sat on the toilet. She should've known explosive diarrhea always signaled her period was coming soon. As she slid the tampon in, she felt a sense of relief wash over her—guilty relief, that left a cold pit in her stomach, because there had been a time the blood didn't come, back when she was younger and not as diligent about condom use. Her emotions got the best of her and she sat on the toilet and wept.

She had tried once before to contact it, to apologize. It never answered her. Wanda had named it Jessie, though she never knew if it was a boy or girl. Sometimes she fancied it was a girl with pigtails in her hair. It was stupid, she knew, and she guessed it would never want an apology from a mother who spread her legs on a cold sterile table to have it removed, to have it killed.

Wanda continued to drink, repeating to herself that it was for the best, but she couldn't shake the thoughts of what its little face would've looked like. She never could say for sure who its daddy was. In her profession it was impossible to know, especially in those years long ago when she also slept with men for pleasure, not just for money. Her irresponsibility cost her. Those days spent at the clinic haunted her at night. She had done many dirty and degrading things in her life, but none of them had held onto her like the decision to terminate the life of her unborn child, especially now that she was getting older and lonelier.

Wanda went to the refrigerator. The beer was almost gone so she opened the cabinet above the stove to retrieve the half bottle of whiskey she had stashed away. It was just about midnight and a thought stuck in her mind: Her grandmother used to say that midnight was the witching hour, the time of ghosts.

"One more time?" she asked herself.

She placed a Ouija board upon the cheap coffee table in her sitting room and hit the lights. The last time she didn't use candles or anything, it was three in the afternoon and she got nothing. This time she was going to follow every step she could remember from movies she'd seen in order to conduct a proper séance. Wanda arranged mulberry-scented candles about the table, and just before her microwave clock read midnight, she pulled Jean Claude's body from the plastic bag. She grabbed a kitchen knife and waited. At the stroke of midnight, she jabbed the rooster's corpse, a pool of red gathering slowly in the hole. Its blood was thickening. She held it upside down, squeezed and shook it like she was trying to get the last drops of ketchup out of the bottle. She shook it some more, dripping its blood all about the witchboard—that's what her grandmother called the Ouija. She said they were of the devil, too, and shouldn't be played with, but the old woman also said oral sex was disgusting, and Wanda definitely knew that was a lie.

The old woman always warned her not to fool around with such evil but she never listened to the pious wind bag, not about sex, not about drugs, and certainly not about God and the devil. Wanda ran away from her over-religious grandmother's house when she was sixteen and became a stripper. She worked at The Pink Beaver for a year before going to work for Jim Dandy. He promised more money and followed through, but she also found herself in a situation she couldn't escape. Twenty years and one abortion later, she found herself sitting on her living room floor, hovering over a dead rooster named Jean Claude Van Damme and a Ouija board, preparing to speak to the spirit of her aborted child.

\*\*\*

Wanda placed her hands upon the small heart-shaped indicator—the instructions called it a planchette—and waited. She felt a little foolish, so she pulled her hands away and picked up her whiskey bottle. She hit it hard and thought for a moment, desperately wondering what to say. Her guts rumbled and burned but she felt the courage to continue.

"I'm tryin' to reach the spirit of my baby," she spoke to the empty trailer.

She placed her hands back over the board, resting her fingertips on the planchette. There was nothing, no movement, no sound.

"Are you there?"

The candles were cheap, like everything else she owned, and they were quickly burning down into pools of crimson wax.

"I wanted to say how sorry I am," she said softly.

Again there was nothing but incredible stillness.

"Will you forgive me? Will you forgive Mama for what she done?"

Her skin grew cold up her back at calling herself *Mama*, and goosebumps rose on her arms. There was no response, but she felt her empty trailer was not empty at all, and the vacuum of silence engulfing her was filled with muted voices.

"Speak to me," Wanda said, and a tear hung at the corner of her eye.

The planchette moved, only slightly, but it did indeed move. She fought the urge to pull her hands away and strained her ears. There, she caught it, a faint exhalation.

"I know you can hear me." Her voice broke.

She watched as her hands moved, guided not by her will but something unseen.

I-H-A-V-E

"What do you have?" she asked.

I-T

"My baby?"

The planchette moved forcefully over the YES.

"Can I speak to it?"

Her hands moved quickly back over the YES.

"Is it all right?"

The planchette moved over to the NO.

Tears fell from her eyes as it spelled H-E-L-P-M-E

"What can I do? How can I help my baby?" she asked.

A cold wind blew into her face and the flames of the candles leapt into the darkness.

"What can I do?" she begged.

N-O-T-H-I-N-G

Wanda pulled her hands away as the planchette spun and darted erratically on its own about the board, spelling gibberish words and repeatedly passing over the number six. She felt a terrible sense of dread, and knew she had fucked up in a big way.

Wanda tried to stand up, wanting nothing more than to take the damn board back to Roy's house, but her legs wouldn't obey the frightened commands of her brain. She recalled then his conversation with her. He'd made her promise not to use it alone. At the time she laughed at him. What was she supposed to do, go ask some trucker who wanted a blow job if he wouldn't mind helping her contact the ghost of her aborted fetus? She realized now she should've heeded his warning, and her grandmother's.

She was dressed only in a Whitesnake t-shirt and a pair of floral-print panties, and she felt like she would freeze to death. The cold was unlike any winter she had ever felt; it was not external, it was more akin to the frigid feeling of dread. It radiated outward from her stomach to the tips of her fingers. The candles snuffed in an instant and that's when it spoke to her.

"It is with me. It belongs to me now."

She felt as if she couldn't breathe. The only light was the moonlight in the window and the red illumination from the clock on her microwave. Shadows moved in every black corner and the floorboards moaned under heavy feet.

"I can give it back to you," the garbled voice spoke, and she jumped at how it seemed to be right beside her ear.

"Mama!" it giggled.

She didn't have the courage to respond. There was heavy breathing at her neck followed by the sensation of the tip of a tongue at her ear. Her skin crawled; it reminded her of the moment before being screwed by someone completely repulsive, and she knew its intent.

Wanda desperately gripped the bottom of her shirt as she felt it begin to be lifted. A black shadow crawled up her thighs and rough hands gripped them, pulling them apart. She released her shirt for just a moment while fighting to push her legs back together and it was torn in two, leaving her bare breasts free in the darkness. Instantly she felt a mouth over her nipple, sucking hard, and sharp teeth nipped the tip of it. Warmth ran from it down onto her flat stomach. The same rough tongue came to claim the falling blood. Her eyes were adjusting to the absence of light, and over her billowed a great shadow, much larger than any man she'd ever seen. Her panties were torn free of her. A hand groped her, and gigantic fingers probed her, fishing her tampon free and flinging the bloody projectile against her TV. She knew better than to fight it; there were too many times she'd had to put her mind somewhere else. That was fairly easy when it came to getting banged by a human, but she was about to be used by something completely demonic and her terror kept her right there on the floor of her trailer, completely cognizant, to experience it all.

Its moaning was animalistic and reminded her of a goat or a sheep. It sucked fist-sized hickies on her thighs. It was forceful, but it seemed to tease her as if it wanted her to enjoy their meeting. A massive tongue slid over her and her body reacted in sickening arousal. The entity radiated a sexual energy, and the longer it hovered over her and played with her naked body, the more she could not hold back from becoming turned on by it. She found herself willingly allowing the demon in, and her mind repeated the same request: "I want my baby back."

"Your wish has been granted," it said, and she couldn't help but feel there would certainly be a price to be paid for her foolishness.

# ADRIANA

SHE CLOSED THE door behind her and screamed at a shadow in the living room. It made her heart leap and beat wildly. Adriana calmed immediately after realizing how small the silhouette was, and knew her grandmother, Consuelo, was sitting on the couch in the near-complete darkness. Their dog sat beside her and she stroked its fur. The old woman lit a small candle; its flame flickered and ate into the wick, casting a yellow glow over her wrinkled face.

"*Te sientes bien?*" Adriana asked.

"*Si, no puedo dormir.*"

Adriana had lived with her grandmother most of her life; after an accident claimed the lives of her mother and brother, it was only she and the old woman. She knew Consuelo too well. The old woman had a reason to be waiting for her. The dog stood up on the couch and a low rumbling growl came from its gut. Adriana felt an alarm inside of her going off. She knew the powers her grandmother held, and if the old woman seemed concerned about something, it meant trouble. The dog leaped off the couch and ran by Adriana. It stood before the door, its short hair standing up in a ridge along its back. She wasn't as adept as her grandmother, but she wasn't blind. It was a bad sign.

Adriana hurried to sit beside her grandmother; she held her hand as a shadow filled the window beside the door. It darted quickly, like a bird in the sky beyond the curtains, only it was large. Consuelo squeezed her granddaughter's hand tightly. The dog started barking and gnashing its teeth at the door. The shadow didn't return, but in the air hung a gut-churning stillness. They sat for what felt like an eternity before the visible tension in the dog's whole body eased. His hair laid back down and he backed away from the door to sit at their feet. Consuelo's grip on Adriana's hand eased too, and they sat in silence. Ever since Adriana was a child she experienced moments like this, when things of nightmares seemed so real. Her grandmother would often apologize but Adriana had become accustomed to it; such was the life of the *curandera*, and her granddaughter had grown to accept it. The atmosphere eased and her grandmother stood up, offering her a hand. Adriana accepted it and embraced the old woman.

"*Ven, mi nina.*"

Consuelo helped Adriana into bed and closed the bedroom door. Her heart was still racing. It had been years since she'd felt so close to death. Consuelo had felt it growing closer and closer to her in recent weeks. Her dreams were becoming filled with visions of powerful men and blood, but tonight they bore the face of a demon. The old woman knew Apache Wells was getting too dangerous for her granddaughter already, but out there in the night someone was dabbling in darkness they didn't understand, and they would pay dearly for it.

# ROY

WANDA AWOKE TO the sound of herself weeping the same pitiful sobs she always experienced when dreaming of the day she gave up her child. She sat up to find she had slept naked on the orange carpet of her living room. Her nipples were erect and irritated, a smear of blood dried across her abdomen. The urgent need to blow chunks sent her running for the kitchen sink. She barely made it, desperately holding her mouth shut. The acidic vomit came out her nostrils first, and she unleashed the rest of it into a sink loaded with dirty dishes. She heaved painfully and emptied her stomach, the contents mostly liquid. The stench of liquor and puke mingled with the scent of dried-up leftover food glued to the dirty dishes, and she heaved again. Her watery eyes opened to survey the damage, and she decided to throw every dish away instead of trying to wash them. A sticky warm blood clot came sliding down her leg, reminding her that she was on her period. She squeezed her legs together to hold back as much blood as she could and made her way awkwardly to the bathroom.

She stood before the mirror, and couldn't remember the last time she'd looked and felt so rough. She sat quickly upon the toilet as another thick clot came seeping out and hung, slightly swaying like a pendulum. It fell into the toilet bowl and she looked down at her thighs. Hickies, the mark of the beast. She still didn't want to believe the night before had actually happened, but she couldn't deny the proof; it was physically imprinted in her pale skin. Golden hairs stood up on her arms as she shook violently. After so many years as a hooker, the old sensation of being tainted came crawling up her back. It was a shame surely brought on by her religious upbringing; she knew sex work wasn't something to feel embarrassed about, but it was a feeling she had suppressed countless times. Her grandmother's voice ate into her, degraded her, wouldn't leave her. She turned and leaned over the side of the tub as a wave of nausea cramped her guts. She was left without satisfaction after dry-heaving a few times. She turned the shower on and forced herself to step into the cold stream of water.

***

Wanda showered and got dressed. She just wanted to clean up her trailer and take the damned Ouija board back to Roy. Her insides twisted with every moment she was alone; the stillness was surrounding her again, but she didn't feel alone and it left her on edge. She pulled yellow rubber gloves up to her elbows and loaded a trash bag with the stinking contents of the sink, then dragged it into the adjoining living room. She peeled and scraped the melted candles off the table, picked up the empty whiskey bottle and beer cans, and crammed it all into the trash bag. She found her shredded t-shirt and underwear beneath the coffee table, and hesitated before touching them. The feeling of her tampon being pulled free came back to her, how its string was yanked tight before it slid free from her. She turned to look at her TV. There was a spatter of menstrual blood and a thin trail down the screen, and the tampon, soaked in brown-red blood, looked like a skinned mouse with a little white tail on the orange carpet. For most of the morning she felt numb, but seeing it made her knees shake once more and the feeling that she seriously fucked up came flooding over her again. She ran to to dispose of it and the memories that came along with it. The last item she hastily shoved into the trash bag was the corpse of Jean Claude Van Damme. He had already begun to stink. The trash wouldn't be picked up for another three days, and she knew it would end up smelling like a gut pile behind a slaughterhouse.

Wanda power-walked the bag out to the can beside her driveway and hurried back inside. She was trying to build the courage to touch the Ouija board, to throw it back in its box, when there was a knock at the door. She knew by the quick procession of light knocks it was Roy.

"Wanda, you home?" he called.

She grabbed the board, threw it into its box, tossed the planchette in on top of it, and pushed the lid down over it.

"Just a minute!" she answered.

"I tried to catch you out by your trash can, but you were too quick for me!" he laughed.

She pulled the door open to see her neighbor standing there. He was a few years older than her, but didn't show it. He wore his dark hair in a ponytail, as well as his usual wife-beater tank-top and black jeans. Most would consider him the unsavory type due to his business ventures, but Wanda never judged him; it seemed ridiculous to look down on him when she sold her ass for cash.

"I came to retrieve my Ouija board from you and ask you if you've seen my cock."

She hesitated, and he laughed.

"My rooster."

"Sure haven't," she answered, rolling her eyes at the innuendo.

"Fuck!"

"Maybe he's out screwin' around with some hens." Wanda smiled.

She opened the door and motioned him inside. He sat down on her sofa; in hip neighborhoods it would've been considered vintage, but in her trailer park it was just the same type of rundown furniture everybody owned.

"Goddammit! I need that fuckin' rooster!"

"He'll come back," she assured him, knowing his money-maker was wrapped in a garbage bag and stuffed down into a mess of vomit-encrusted dishes. "Don't you have any more?"

"Sure I do, but not like Jean Claude," Roy said. He leaned forward and tapped his fingers on the Ouija board box. "Any luck?"

"Nope," she said.

"You didn't use it alone, right?"

"No. A lady I work with came over," she lied.

"That's good. Sometimes bad things come through, and you don't want to be alone if that happens."

"What could happen?" she asked.

"Ever watch *The Exorcist?*"

She shook her head, but she could guess what he was getting at. "No."

"Little girl gets possessed by a demon using one of these alone," he said.

She could feel the hair rise on her arms. "Scary."

"Yeah, it's a classic."

"Why do you have one, then?" she asked.

"I collect horror movies, creepy stuff, it's just my thing," Roy said.

"And the roosters? Do you host cockfights, or what?"

"Those are just my income," he said, and she could see he wasn't willing to elaborate so she just smiled.

He looked at his watch and jumped from his seat.

"Gotta run, business, ya know." He winked and made his way out the door.

She watched him leave, and felt a mixture of guilt for lying to him and arousal at his scent. She caught herself daydreaming for a second about taking off his clothes and instantly shook the thought from her mind. Her body ached in a strange way, like a mixture of intense sexual excitement and starving to death.

"What the fuck is happening to me?"

Wanda turned back to stare into her empty trailer, but something was there, working its way into her mind.

\*\*\*

She couldn't stand being in her trailer alone so she grabbed her work clothes, shoved them down into her big-ass purse, and headed for the shopping center across the highway from Charlie's Truck Stop. She needed to take her mind off the feeling of being watched and she hoped in a public place it would leave her. She chose to wear red wedge heels to match the dress she would be sporting while working down at the truck stop later in the evening. They were much more comfortable on the blisters left behind from the silver pumps she wore the night before. She always took the alleyway behind Roy's trailer this time of day, hoping to avoid Gene and his habit of trying to accuse her of "owing" him. Her tongue was in no mood for her landlord's hairy asshole, even in the sexually frustrated state she found herself in. The thoughts of it nearly caused her to sprint the whole way to safety.

# DEVIL SHIT

HECTOR SAT AT the table, his father's voice droning on and on in the periphery of his mind. The old man certainly liked to judge him for what he did for a living, but never when Hector came by to leave him extra spending money. Hector's hand strayed under the table to his pocket, and the small bags containing what he would describe as "devil shit." His mind fought back the memory of Gusano and the twin sisters. They were like something out of a horror movie, things that guns and bullets couldn't take down. He found himself wondering if he had chosen the right side in the battle to come, but was sure Chamuco would come out victorious, especially with his allies in black magic. Hector shuttered; Chamuco's rival, Cuervo, was an old-school *narco*, he didn't fuck around, and the price of betrayal would be death. He didn't want to get on Chamuco's bad side, to end up a corpse attached to a rusted piece of wire.

When Chamuco returned from Mexico with the three witches, Hector was appalled by their presence. There was something unnatural about them, something not human in their eyes. Hector never spoke a word about his unease, but he could tell Chamuco's right-hand man, David, felt the same way. David did get vocal about it, but only when the *Tres Gusanos* weren't within ear shot of him, and that spoke volumes to Hector.

The old man had a small television in the kitchen to watch while he made their breakfast, and on the screen flashed the picture of a local priest. Hector scrambled for the remote and turned the volume up until his father's bitching was drowned out by a report of finding the holy man's corpse. His insides grew cold; he knew the priest's name had to have been written on the slip of paper in the envelope he handed Gusano along with the instructions to tamper with the cockfight. His fear solidified his decision to stay in Chamuco's growing army. His lips would remain shut, he would do as he was ordered.

"*Estas sordo, o que?*" his father asked.

"*Relajate,*" Hector said.

His eyes were fixed on the picture of the priest, his gentle eyes and smile. It reminded Hector of his father who, even though still talking shit to him, had always been a kind, loving dad It twisted Hector's gut, made him nauseated, and reminded him he had more than his own life to lose if he found himself on the wrong side of the coming war.

The old man put a plate on the table in front of him and turned back to the stove. Hector didn't feel like eating anymore, but he knew his father would complain if he didn't, so he dug in and tried to banish the worry from his mind.

\*\*\*

His father was on the front porch watering his plants when Hector pulled out of the driveway with a pocket full of devil shit and a belly full of chorizo. Hector glanced in the rearview mirror, hoping he still looked like a tough guy after feeling shaken by the news of the decapitated priest. He had a job to do if he wanted to keep his head on his shoulders and he knew the place to start. He needed to see the prize fighter guru, the papa of the best roosters this side of the border: a white boy named Roy.

# BAD OMEN

ROY OPENED THE box. The board was speckled with crimson. He set about cleaning it; he hated it when a borrowed item came back in worse condition than when he loaned it. He waited by the living room window; Hector would be by any minute looking for Jean Claude. His mind drifted to his money-maker, wondering if the enormous red bastard was still alive. He scratched what he knew to be candle wax off the Ouija board, but there were other stains, and if he didn't know any better, he would swear they were blood.

The rumble of an engine outside caused his balls to jump; Hector would soon be at his door. He dropped the Ouija board onto the sofa and went to a tiny closet beside his front door. He pushed aside two black sweaters and shoved his hand into the pocket of a brown jacket, where his palm met cold steel. He slid the thirty-eight special into the back of his pants and waited. The rumble grew louder until it seemed as though it might rattle the door from its hinges. Hector drove a muscle car and Roy could hear it coming from the moment it entered the trailer park, its bored-out engine roared louder as he made his way closer until it sounded like Armageddon was unleashed in Roy's driveway. The engine died and his anticipation of Hector's knocks at the door knotted his gut.

Hector was an erratic sort of dude known to snap at people, and Roy wasn't one to be fucked with either, so the whole situation had the potential of ending in a very bloody manner. He snuck a look out the peephole to see Hector quick-stepping his way to the door. He walked in a way some might describe as very *cholo*, but he dressed more like a greaser. He swung his tattooed arms while one leg seemed to be constantly trying to catch up to the other; in Roy's eyes, he looked like a chimp with a pompadour. The heavy knocks were followed by Hector's usual greeting.

"Open up, white boy!"

Roy hesitated, and though he told himself about a thousand times that morning he wasn't afraid of no short little Mexican, he knew it was more to try to convince himself since it wasn't entirely true. He feared Hector because he could never gauge what his reaction would be in certain situations. Losing Jean Claude was just one of those, and Roy found himself scrambling for an explanation. He pulled the door open slowly and saw Hector was smiling, which wasn't necessarily a good thing.

"What's up?" Roy asked.

"Whattchu mean?" Hector said. "I'm here for the killer."

"Which one?"

"Don't play stupid, white boy. Jean Claude, I'm here for him."

Roy hesitated again.

"Don't tell me you lost him."

"No, no, he's around here somewhere," Roy lied.

"He better fuckin' be."

"I mean, I haven't seen him, but I know he's here."

Hector shook his head and sniffed the air.

"What's that fuckin' smell, man?" Hector asked. "You take a shower today?"

"What smell?" Roy asked, but his nostrils caught it then. His insides grew cold. It was a familiar smell to a guy who had worked with roosters most of his adult life.

"Smells fuckin' nasty out here. Let me in!"

Roy had no choice but to allow Hector in; if he didn't, it would surely appear as though he had something to hide.

Hector, of course, made himself at home and went directly to the sofa, nearly sitting on the Ouija board.

"Talkin' to the spirits?" Hector teased, but it felt forced and Roy knew the situation was about to turn very serious.

"You're going to have some close-up conversations with them when Chamuco gets you."

"Don't threaten me, Hector. I will find the fuckin' rooster," Roy said.

"So you did lose him?"

Roy nodded apprehensively, his mind replaying his shock at finding the cage had a rooster-sized hole in the wire holding the door together, and no Jean Claude. It wasn't the first time one of his roosters escaped, but since this one was so important, he was positive he would never find him because so often life seemed to like to fuck Roy. This felt eerily like one of those occasions.

"You fuckin' idiot."

"Hey, he's gotten out before and always came back! So calm the fuck down."

For a moment, Hector sat stroking his goatee, his eyes on Roy, and Roy knew he should've tried a different approach.

"It's going to be really tough to act like a hardass without a head on your shoulders, *pendejo!*"

Roy could feel the cold steel of his own pistol against his back where it was hidden under his shirt, and the thoughts of an impending shoot out threatened to turn his bowels to water. His hands were in front of him and he knew if he made a move for his gun, Hector would draw his own and fill his guts with lead before he could get a shot off.

"We know you play both sides of the field, you deal with Cuervo too, do him favors and shit. Maybe you let the rooster go on purpose."

"Cuervo has been the boss for years, not my boss really, but your boss! I'm just the guy who takes care of the roosters. I'm an independent contractor. I wouldn't make any money off being a shady bastard."

"Yeah, I remember you just play with everyone's cocks all day, but I'm serious."

"Real funny, always cock references with you."

Hector pulled his gun and pointed it at Roy's head, "Shit is changin', and you know the sayin': there ain't enough room in this town for two bosses. The pact is ending, and if it wasn't for the rooster you'd probably already be dead. Get out there and look for it."

"Take it easy, I'll find it. And tell Chamuco I'm only loyal to whoever pays me, so he can forget about taking me out over a dispute with Cuervo," Roy said.

"You're a pussy!"

"No, I'm a businessman," Roy said.

"That's more like it, *maricon.*"

Hector stood and motioned to the door. "Let's go."

"Where?" Roy asked, trying to avoid any long rides with a known cartel member.

"To find the killer, you dumb hillbilly!"

Roy nodded and took a step, then hesitated. Hector wanted him to walk in front of him, and for a second Roy wondered if he was going to be shot in the back.

"Get moving, the longer this takes, the less forgiving *mi jefe* becomes," Hector said, and for a moment Roy almost joked as to which boss he was referring to but decided his sarcasm would only end up getting him killed. Besides, he wasn't lying when he said he was loyal only to those who paid him. He'd cut the throat of Cuervo or Chamuco for the right wad of cash and leave them in the desert for the vultures to devour.

\*\*\*

They were standing in Roy's backyard. Hector was looking into each separate pen the white boy was using to house his roosters, but Jean Claude Van Damme was nowhere to be seen. Roy could tell by the way Hector rambled strings of curses in Spanish that he was in a dire situation.

"You will lose some fingers for this, I can guarantee. You'll be lucky if they let you live."

The smell from earlier came drifting through the backyard and Roy decided honesty may be the best way to go; a few fingers being cut off would be better than having his head sawed off.

"Don't you smell that?" he asked, and Hector froze. "It's death."

"You're going to be if that smell is the killer," Hector said.

Roy followed his nose around the side of his trailer and passed a broken-down station wagon he had been wrenching on. Its intensity grew, and though it turned his stomach he took long deep sniffs in hopes of locating the source.

"Probably got ran over, you fuckin' idiot!" Hector said.

"No. I would've found evidence," Roy said.

"Like feathers?" Hector asked.

"Yes, like that." Roy was tired of the psycho Mexican plaguing him for the last hour.

Hector stepped into Wanda's yard and picked up a wad of crimson feathers.

"Stupid whore!" Roy muttered, but he didn't want to believe it.

The stains on his Ouija board came back to him, and he clenched his fists. The stink was unmistakable, and they followed it to her trash can.

"He's in there," Hector said.

Roy lifted the lid and the stench slapped him in the face. He envisioned her slathering his money-maker's blood all over the witchboard in an attempt to speak with the spirit of her lost child. Hector lifted the trash bag and shoved it into Roy's chest.

"Open it."

Roy did as he was told, pulling the bag open, and there, reeking of death and vomit, was Jean Claude Van Damme's corpse in the beginning stages of decay. Hector turned and heaved onto the sidewalk. His chorizo breakfast stained the cracked concrete a bright red-orange.

"What do we do?" Roy asked, though he knew the answer.

Hector's cellphone rang. They looked to each other, exchanging a terrified glance. Hector answered it with a trembling hand. His usual cocky attitude wasn't present at all to whomever he spoke to so Roy knew it had to be Chamuco, his new boss.

"He knows, doesn't he?" Roy asked in disbelief. "How the fuck does he already know?"

Hector nodded, his face serious. "Gusano told him, and he gave me my orders."

"Who the fuck is Gusano, is he fuckin' psychic?"

"He's a *brujo*, motherfucker! He knows shit!"

"He's a what?" Roy asked.

"You don't want to know," Hector said.

"What did he say?"

"This bitch has to pay. It's her or you, white boy! Make your choice," Hector said.

"Let's go!" said Roy.

Something in his gut felt sorry for Wanda, but he knew if she wasn't dealt with, he'd find himself in the back freezer of a *carniceria* waiting to have his knees broken and his face forced into a meat grinder.

# MOMMY

THE THRIFT STORE smelled like an apple-cinnamon candle, as always. Wanda's arm was draped with four dresses she thought would be good work outfits. She was making her way to the fitting rooms when she heard a familiar voice.

"Think those will make a difference?"

Carla was smirking and twirling a strand of her long red hair around her finger. She chomped a piece of gum like a cow chewing its cud. Wanda held up her middle finger and the younger whore giggled.

"Old hoes like you are really sad! I'm only doing this until I finish cosmetology school, then me and Jim are moving to Florida together."

Wanda was sick of Carla always implying she really gave a fuck about Jim anymore. She would be happy to see his albino ass go.

"You can have that milky douchebag "

Carla rolled her eyes and strutted away while Wanda seethed. She really wanted to ask where Carla succeeded in slaying the lime green zebra she fashioned into her obnoxious jumpsuit, but she held her tongue. She could feel sooner or later they would end up in a bitch fight in the parking lot of the truck stop but she really didn't feel like getting arrested...again. It would probably mean she would have to blow Sheriff Lancaster...again.

\*\*\*

Wanda located an empty dressing room, closed its flimsy door behind her, and got undressed. She looked herself over in the floor-length mirror. In the harsh lights of the thrift store her reflection looked haggard. She stepped closer to examine the hickies on her thighs—they were more like bruises, but there were obvious tooth marks left behind, and they definitely weren't human. She gripped the fat of her thigh and twisted it slightly in an attempt to get a better view. She was nearly touching the mirror when she heard a sound like someone sighing faintly. She felt chilly standing almost naked in the dressing room, her bare feet like ice against the tile floor. A draft swept up her back and her skin instantly rose in gooseflesh. She was not alone; whatever she'd encountered in her trailer had followed her to the thrift store, and would continue to do so wherever she went. The mirror showed only her ragged reflection, but she felt a presence at her back. She didn't dare move—her mind was screaming for her to run, but she couldn't bring her body to respond.

The three old women who worked at the thrift store were well aware of Wanda's profession and treated her like a strung-out crack whore. If she ran out of a dressing room without her clothes on, they would surely call the police. Wanda was frantic now as the air around her seemed to breathe. A tear slid down her cheek when what felt like a tiny, cold hand gripped hers. She pulled her eyes away from the mirror and looked down at her frigid hand. There appeared to be nothing there, nothing her eyes could see at least. She heard the faint sigh again and glanced back to the mirror to see a twisted shadowy form holding onto her fingers. She couldn't scream. Her voice was forced back into her throat when she realized her visitor was the size of a child. Her heart seized in her chest, and when it returned to beating it was intensely painful.

"My baby?" she whispered.

The form tightened its grip on her and a voice spoke.

"Mommy!"

Her mouth fell open at the sound of it, for it was not childlike.

She tugged her hand away and found herself trapped in the far corner of the tiny dressing room. The shadow loomed before her, blocking her escape.

\*\*\*

She was huddling in her underwear, watching as the being came crawling over her. It felt like a thousand spiders scurrying over her skin.

"No!" she screamed.

A guttural voice mocked her pleas. "No, no, no."

She kicked and punched feebly, unable to shake the presence steadily wrapping about her like a cocoon.

There was a knocking at the dressing room door: one of the old hags who worked for the thrift store. "Hello? What are you doing in there?"

"Help me! It's getting me!" Wanda cried.

"You're alone in there, I can see your feet!" the old woman answered.

The old woman stuck her head under the door, adjusting her glasses. "You're alone! Are you on drugs?"

Wanda's ears were filled with demonic voices laughing at her distress and crying like newborn babies. The shadows were dissipating, but Wanda knew the old woman could not see them. A sudden pain tore through her abdomen; then her vagina cramped and her tampon slid free in her underwear. Embarrassment and terror flooded her. She looked to the mirror to see her panties filling with blood and tiny spectral arms protruding from her twat. .

"I'm gonna call the police if you don't get out of here!" the old woman warned.

Wanda was fixated at the sight in the mirror and began to weep.

"Get your damn clothes on and get out!"

She didn't answer the hysterical old bitch. Through her tears she watched the ghostly infant arms receding back into her.

"GET OUT!" The woman was screaming.

Wanda stood and pulled her clothes on, unable to reinsert another tampon, and fled into the sunlit parking lot.

# IT'S HER OR YOU

WANDA SAT ON the curb behind the burger joint in the thrift store parking lot. She had already smoked two packs of cigarettes, but refrained from eating, not wishing to have another hobo bath in the truck stop sink. She was ragging it and the thoughts of going to work in her state made her want to hitchhike as far from Jim Dandy as she could. It would be a red wing night.

She looked at her watch—she had a few hours to kill before her shift started, but there was nowhere to go. She decided to get up and walk over to the truck stop and buy a pack of crackers to calm her stomach and take some Midol to help with her cramps. Her thoughts were on what was happening to her, the things she had seen. She didn't even notice the rumbling of an engine behind her.

***

"When I said a whore I meant a fuckin' hooker," Roy said. "Maybe she works the lot at Charlie's."

"Excuse me, *pendejo*. I never pay for pussy. I thought maybe she worked at The Pink Beaver."

"Go back to the truck stop, we're wasting time!" Roy said.

They had been on the hunt for Wanda for over an hour, searching seedy street corners for any sign of her. Roy was beyond irritated when Hector decided to search for her in the local nudie bar; the stint took up half an hour when the owner recognized Hector and offered him free lap dances.

"I don't think the boss would be happy about wasting time in a strip club," Roy fumed.

"That was about business, white boy. You don't understand that, when offers are made to show you respect you take them," Hector said. "Maybe you know nothing about respect or business, but I do!"

"Let's just find this bitch," Roy said.

"We will. That's a promise."

"What are we going to do when we find her?"

Hector looked to him and raised an eyebrow. "She has to speak to the *jefe*."

"Which one?"

"Cuervo."

"Cuervo? I thought this was Chamuco's rooster?" Roy asked.

"It is, hillbilly, but I have a mission to complete in that *carniceria*. So we're gonna pretend she was just a rat bitch and Cuervo's men will take care of her. He'll find out soon enough what Chamuco plans to do with him."

"What're they gonna do to *her*?"

"Don't turn into a pussy! I can take you to see El Cuervo instead, and tell him you're a rat too."

Roy shook his head. "I'm not going down for this."

Hector was driving erratically as he dug in his pocket. He fished out a black sack and then a red one and threw them on the dashboard. "Get this shit outta my pocket before my balls get cursed or something."

"What the hell is that?" Roy asked as he reached out, but Hector slapped his hand away.

"Don't touch that, white boy. That's some devil shit."

"What? Like black magic bullshit?"

"It's something I was ordered to put on the killer, to make sure he won the fight. And the other is for Cuervo's little bitch chicken. Red bag equals good shit, black bag equals bad shit. Chamuco wanted to humiliate Cuervo a little bit before taking his throne. You know all that macho shit. Chamuco wants to make him look like an old *puto* in front of his men, and we all know how obsessed Cuervo is with the roosters, how he mysteriously never loses."

"That plan is out the window since this bitch killed my rooster," Roy said.

"Yeah, but Chamuco changed the game plan. Cuervo don't know about the killer being dead, and by now he's getting word there's war on the horizon. He's probably making plans of his own and shit, ya feel me? The cockfight will still be the beginning of it all so I have my orders from above to fulfill."

"Why are you telling me all this shit?"

"Because dead men don't tell secrets, and I needed to make a confession before the war commences. We'll probably both be dead by midnight..."

"That's reassuring."

"Actually, I want you on board with this change of authority. We've gotten along most of the time, you're a good little bitch and maybe we can throw jobs your way besides just stroking cocks." Hector giggled a bit, he couldn't resist the innuendo.

"Such a comedian."

"You know, we could use a white-bread hillbilly like you, you wouldn't raise the suspicions of the *chorizo* on *la frontera*. I already asked Chamuco about you and he gave me the okay, but that's only if we live through this shit with the rooster."

"Why would I want to work with him?"

"You don't want to turn Chamuco down. He's a scary motherfucker, deals with the devil and all that. If you saw the shit around him that I have, you'd just say, *si patron*, and do whatever he tells you."

Hector's hand strayed to the blister on his chest from the crucifix he wore as protection.

"I don't believe in shit like witchcraft, but I'm not looking to get my ass shot off either."

"So, is that a yes, *puto*?"

Roy didn't answer. He just shook his head and kept staring out the window.

Evening was coming and Roy spotted her sitting on the curb behind Fast Burger. He pointed her out, but immediately a pang of guilt rang in his gut. "There she is."

He felt like an executioner, like a real piece of shit, but he didn't have any other choice.

# CUERVO

SHERIFF LANCASTER GLANCED over his shoulder before making his way into the Rancho Grande Carniceria and Mercado. He made his way up a side aisle. The meat counter was busy with people shouting their orders and crowding the display case, but he wasn't there to purchase anything. The sheriff was there to meet with Cuervo; he had some news to impart to his longtime associate. At the back end of the store was a door posted for employees only; he knew Cuervo would be in the back somewhere, probably already fuming over the priest's death. He pushed through the door and found his way into the inner sanctum of the *carniceria*, where the real business took place. The back warehouse was enormous and had a large walk-in freezer, a place the sheriff hoped to never see the inside of—they kept more than animal meat in there. At the far end there was a roll-up door large enough to accommodate big trucks hauling in meat, vegetables, and, of course, contraband from all over Mexico and the United States. The man he sought was just beside it.

Cuervo was sitting at a large stainless-steel table, his eyes dark with what Sheriff Lancaster knew was rage. They had been friends and business associates for more than twenty years, long before Chamuco's uncle came and split the territory in two and gave half to his nephew. Sheriff Lancaster had a very sweet deal for many years, turning a blind eye to the trucks hauling Cuervo's merch, and as long as the cartel kept any killings out beyond the city lights of Apache Wells, the sheriff would stay out of it in exchange for a hefty chunk of cash every month. He was concerned with the new order of things, but his suspicions were confirmed when Chamuco began breaking the long-time agreement he had with Cuervo.

"Hey, partner. I guess you've already watched the news?" he said.

"Of course I have, asshole. Why didn't you protect him?"

"Hey now, wait just a damn minute. You told me there was a truce, a pact of no violence. How was I supposed to know the priest was in danger?"

Cuervo ran his hand over his face and nodded. "You're right."

"Who did this? Boys from the south or the asshole you presently have as a neighbor?" the sheriff asked

"I suspect it to be the little piece of shit Chamuco," Cuervo said, and laid his pistol on the table.

"What's your plans for this guy, Cuervo? This shit can't continue, he's been taking people out left and right and making it look like I can't do my job."

"Up until this point he'd only killed his own people, but now he's crossed the line. The priest, before he died, relayed a message to me."

"And? What did he say?" Sheriff Lancaster asked.

"He said one of Chamuco's trusted men came to him and warned him there was going to be war."

"Fuck! This town is gonna burn, what are you gonna do?"

"I'm going to bide my time, pretend like I know nothing, but then I'm going to hit him hard."

"And when exactly is that gonna happen?"

"One day, no more than that. There's gonna be a meeting for the territories here and the ones from down south. He plans to make me look bad during a cockfight, but I have a surprise for him. He won't walk out of that meeting alive."

"Cockfighting? Cartel wars? What else am I gonna have to cover up?"

"You won't have to cover up shit. It's going to be on the outskirts as we agreed. He's going to simply drive into the desert and never return."

"Okay, I like the sound of that. Just keep it far away from town, that's all I ask," Sheriff Lancaster said.

Cuervo stood up and shook his hand. "You have my word."

A horn honked on the other side of the roll-up door and Cuervo motioned for the sheriff to leave. "I have business to attend to. I'll call you later."

"All right, but remember the agreement," the sheriff warned, and walked away.

Cuervo's men told him it was Hector at the door. Cuervo smiled and wondered how Chamuco would like to have Hector's body sent back to him without a head. It would be like a match dropped in a pool of gasoline, but Cuervo welcomed it. He didn't want his rival to think he wouldn't retaliate for the death of Padre Guillermo. He wanted to continue the charade of pretending to be unaware of Chamuco's plans, but having one of his rival's men so close to the freezer was too much for

Cuervo to pass up. He would gamble on it; by the time Chamuco realized Hector's fate, the war would already be started and it wouldn't matter.

# THE FREEZER

THE EXPLOSION OF pain at the back of her skull left her temporarily blinded, and though one of the voices seemed familiar, it was muffled in her ears. Wanda could feel herself being lifted up from the gritty asphalt and tossed into a small space. The failing light went completely black as a lid was shut over her. It felt as if she was thrown into a coffin until the roar of an engine filled her ears and she realized she was in the trunk of a car. The smell of gasoline and blood filled her nose, and her body shifted and slid as the car maneuvered, accelerated, and slowed down. The back of her head was warm and wet when she brought her hand to the stinging wound. She screamed and punched the heavy steel trunk lid, only to bust her knuckles open. Terror seized her—not from her abduction, but from being trapped in complete darkness with the entity wrapping itself about her once more.

"Mommy." It spoke in the same mocking voice, turning her stomach; the voice of the beast.

She wept as she felt her body painfully contorting against her will. Something cold moved beneath her skin, taking hold of her and forcing her true self into a tiny corner of her mind.

\*\*\*

The Rancho Grande Carniceria was on the outskirts of town. It was the only Hispanic supermarket within thirty miles; El Cuervo made sure of it. Its outward appearance spoke of the owner's pride of his heritage, beautifully decorated with treasures crafted by the artisans of Mexico. The front shopping area smelled of fresh bread from the *panaderia* and rich spices sold for cooking traditional dishes. Colorful pinatas hung from the ceiling, and the cashiers were beautiful young Hispanic women. Hector and Roy did not enter through the front, but instead they were met at the back door, one made of solid steel with a small bulletproof-glass window serving as a peephole for the men on the other side.

"We have a delivery," Hector said to the window, a code of sorts.

"A delivery of what?" the man on the other side asked.

"*Carne*," Hector answered.

Roy understood a little Spanish, enough to know that Hector had said "meat."

There was a sound to their right, and that's when Roy noticed they were standing beside a huge garage door. It clinked as it began to open.

"Get back in the car," Hector said.

Roy went to sit in the passenger seat while Hector continued his conversation with the doorman in Spanish. The trunk was silent, and for that he was grateful. He had heard her struggle a bit at first, but now she was quiet. He envisioned her trapped in the dark trunk, scared to death. His gut twisted with guilt, a guilt he had been fighting for hours. It wasn't really her fault; he was the one who forgot to secure Jean Claude's cage. He thought about her confessing her guilt about "taking care" of her pregnancy to him, begging him to borrow his Ouija board. She was nothing more than a pitiful whore. He turned to see Hector walking towards the car. There was no time now to turn back; they were going to meet El Cuervo, and he would decide Wanda's fate. Roy could only hope she got out of this with a few broken bones, and not wrapped in plastic in the meat freezer.

"What are you lookin' at, white boy?" Hector asked.

"Nothin'," Roy answered.

"You look like you're gonna pussy out. Just remember, El Chamuco doesn't like pussies."

"I know Cuervo don't like traitors either..." Roy said.

"He won't do shit, he has no idea who is on his side. He's old school, he'll want to confront Chamuco *cara a cara*, face to face, like men."

"He has eyes and ears everywhere, he could know that you plan to help Chamuco too."

"Chamuco has more than that," Hector said.

\*\*\*

Hector shoved the red and black sacks into his pocket and drove into the warehouse, the garage door closing quickly behind them. They were met by a group of younger men; all were dressed similar to Hector, and Roy wondered what gang they were affiliated with. He had seen the groups of *cholos* who usually ran the streets, but these men were different. They didn't wear baggy pants and oversized t-shirts; they wore flashy Western-style clothing and pointed-toe boots tipped in silver. He swallowed the lump in his throat when he realized these were obviously cartel members straight out of old Mexico. They spoke Spanish so quickly he could only decipher a few words, and he figured they used lots of slang, so he didn't even try to guess what was said. There were four of them, but one did most of the talking. Hector was busy nodding his head and his voice sounded very agreeable. Roy recognized something in his associate—fear—and a crazy motherfucker like Hector being afraid put Roy on the verge of a stroke. He prayed Cuervo hadn't already gotten wind of Chamuco's plans to exterminate him, because being in the company of Hector would look very bad for Roy, traitorous in fact.

"Help me take her into the freezer," Hector said.

*** 

Roy was sickened by her appearance. There was an odor of dead fish and shit permeating the trunk. They lifted her—Roy held her arms while Hector grabbed her feet—and she was like a bag of bones. Her skin felt loose, and her appendages were floppy; Roy would've guessed her dead if it weren't for the gentle rising of her chest. The other men led them quickly along the back warehouse wall. This was a new side of the Mexican mercado, a dirty contrast to its bright colorful shopping area. The lighting gave off a soft blue glow and the white walls reminded Roy of some kind of hospital or institution. He wanted nothing more than to get the fuck out of there, his nerves were shot and he was feeling overwhelming guilt. They stopped before a stainless-steel freezer door. The men in the pointed-toe boots spoke to Hector once more and he emphatically nodded. The door was pulled open and Hector went in first; apparently this wasn't his first visit to the freezer. Roy followed behind him while the others waited.

"We have to take her all the way to the back," Hector instructed.

"What are they going to do?" Roy asked.

"I never know the answer to that. I just leave them," Hector said, confirming Roy's suspicions.

"I mean, they won't...kill her. Right?"

Hector didn't say a word.

They found themselves at the farthest end of the freezer. It was stacked with various cuts of meat on stainless-steel tables. They hoisted her onto an empty table. Roy's arms and knees felt like rubber, but his brain screamed for him to get out of that place that reeked of frozen blood.

"*Hola, muchachos,*" came a deep voice from behind them.

They turned, and Roy watched Hector grin widely, but in the matter of a second that smile faded.

"El Cuervo, *el mero mero,*" Hector said in introduction.

Roy offered his hand, but the suave older man didn't shake it, and that's when he knew he was fucked. There was a hot explosion in his chest, and for a moment he thought he had been shot, like his chest had caught fire. It caused him to piss his pants and convulse, but the current running through his body was no bullet—he had been zapped with a Taser. He fell to the cold floor and struggled to regain control of his body. There was a commotion, and he could hear an argument in Spanish; then Hector fell beside him. Cuervo had already figured out that Chamuco planned mutiny, and he meant to end it with bullets and blood. Roy readied himself to die. All he could see coming at him were booted feet, toes tipped in silver and shining in the white light of the freezer.

# BIRTH

IT CONTROLLED HER flesh and bones. She was in there somewhere, lost within her own mind. She sat forward by their command, her joints loose and rubbery. With a wet crunching of bones sliding from sockets and cords of muscle shifting, she watched from a faraway place as her body contorted into something. It crawled like an insect on broken elbows and twisted kneecaps. Her skirt was hiked up, and from beneath her bloodstained panties a hot exhalation of breath hung in a cloud. She wanted to cry, but it would not allow it; it needed her eyes to see its new surroundings. The spirit residing inside of her was agitated by the cold and calculated its escape from the freezer. Her head flopped back at an unnatural angle so it could see behind them; her human eyes were becoming useless compared to the cluster of them forming just above her pubic bone, black and lidless. Rows of teeth serrated their way through her soft vaginal skin, forming what appeared to be the sideways mouth of a shark. The flesh holding the eye-cluster ballooned outward, forming the upper portion of a small face. The demons were satisfied with the transformation of the human woman, so they instructed her new frame to walk. It struggled for a moment like a newborn foal, until it mastered its new gait and slid off the edge of the cold steel table. It could smell cold meat all around it, but it sensed warm blood in the vicinity, and the urgency to feed became insatiable.

\*\*\*

He was woken up by a wet crunching sound followed by wheezing. Roy opened one swollen eye to see nothing but white incandescent light and the mist of his own breath. The sound grew louder, and a pitiful moaning filled him with terror. He attempted to pull himself up from the floor only to find his cheek was stuck painfully in a pool of his own frozen blood. His hand came across a wad of what felt like cloth, and he held it out to see Hector's sacks of "devil shit." Roy shoved them into his shirt pocket and tried to focus, but pain and confusion clouded his mind. He found that he now only had one good eye, the other having been blinded by the toe of a boot. Not far from him he could see Hector, his mouth hanging open and his chest rising and falling slowly. He realized that was where some of the sounds were coming from. Roy didn't dare speak as his brain fought to understand what was happening. Were they sawing Hector up right beside him?

The crunching continued, and blood came running out of Hector's mouth. There was a contented sigh, humanlike and vaguely close to the sound of a woman in ecstasy. But something about it was different. From his position, he could only see Hector's upper body, but Roy guessed somewhere close by Wanda had either just awakened, or was "buying" her way out of the freezer. He grew angry, suspecting the whore was blowing her way to freedom while he and Hector would be ground up and fed to the opening act of ravenous stray dogs at the next cockfight. A wet ripping filled his ears, and blood rocketed from Hector's mouth, drenching Roy's face. His arms felt like Jell-O as he rolled to his side, trying to lift himself up, but Hector's warm blood lubricated his cheek and he was able to peel it from the floor. He marveled momentarily at the skin he left behind, then brought his shaking hand to his facial wound and prepared to face his attackers once more. Except he wasn't met by the men and their boots, but by a twisted mound of flesh riding Hector.

# ESCAPE

ROY PUSHED HIMSELF backwards across the floor as he watched what looked like Wanda—only her limbs were twisted, and her head hung back as if her neck was broken. Her skirt was rolled up to her belly button and she was straddling Hector, who was naked from the waist down. She rode him, though Roy doubted that the obviously dying man could achieve an erection. He felt bile in his throat when he realized Hector's legs had been completely severed from his body and stripped of their clothing and flesh. Wanda moaned and ran her twisted hands over her body, freeing her breasts from the flimsy shirt covering them. She forced herself down hard and blood came spilling out beneath her. He noticed the cluster of eyes, the face above her twat. Roy scurried away to hide behind an assortment of hanging meats. His mind couldn't fathom the nightmare he had awoken to. The Wanda-creature twisted its body; her head was upside down, and her pale eyes fell on Roy as he peeked between two cow halves.

***

As it pulled itself up off Hector, Roy got a good view of the gore beneath, the rows of teeth still chewing a chunk of the dead man's flaccid, mutilated cock and balls. The black eyes turned upon him and he panicked. It was clear that he had been spotted, and his wobbly legs carried him quickly back to the steel door of the freezer. He placed his back against it and searched the rows of hanging animal corpses for a sign of her...of it. His cheek was raw and his heart beat erratically, and when he heard it a new warmth ran down the leg of his Levis. He didn't have time to be concerned with pissing himself, it was coming his way. It was all bent and contorted, walking like a spider on Wanda's hands and feet. Those black eyes and that twat mouth lined with razors were fixed on him, and all he could think to do was beat the steel door and finally allow himself to scream. His pleas came out harsh and desperate; his body was growing numb from the cold. The adrenaline kept his blood hot and his mind racing, but now he wished El Cuervo had just shot him dead. He screamed once more as the thing that was once Wanda advanced upon him, flipping its back-half over to walk like a human on two feet. He could hear the shifting of her bones momentarily before she leapt at him with her arms outstretched. He kicked her in the chest and she recoiled, only to regain her awkward stance. Her skirt was still rolled up, revealing the hideous, childlike face above her crotch. Its cunt-mouth frothed and snapped, which gave him an idea. He hauled off and booted her right between the legs, in what appeared to be controlling the rest of her spindly body. One of the lidless eyes burst, and a scream issued forth from the greedy maw of her vagina. It was piercing, like the wailing of an infant or an injured cat.

\*\*\*

The cries echoed down the hallway and shook Juan's insides. He already felt like two cats had been fighting in his stomach all day. "El Crudo" was his nickname, because he was cursed with a hangover seven days of the week. He had tried to give up his nightly binges, but never succeeded. He was hired to do odd jobs around the *carniceria*, mostly cleaning and meat cutting. He never questioned the selection of meats in the back freezer, he knew it would be a fatal mistake...but tonight the crying of an infant brought him to the freezer door. He understood most English, but in this case he didn't have to. It was obvious there was a gringo locked in there. Juan didn't give a fuck about him, but the baby. He slid the master key into the padlock and quickly unlocked it, then braced himself for whatever horrible scene he might encounter and opened the door. He was met with a cold breeze and billowing white clouds followed by a lunatic gringo.

\*\*\*

The beast leaped at Roy and grappled with him. It attempted to wrap its legs around his hips in order to pull him into those flapping, teeth-lined pussy lips. He punched the soft windpipe of Wanda's exposed throat, and its grip loosened. He forced the snapping mouth away from his abdomen and, for a second as he slid free, his balls leapt into his throat and his dick receded like the head of a frightened turtle at his proximity to the hungry poon-beast. He shoved free of her and she slid down his leg, twining her legs tightly about it. His jeans shredded beneath the rabid assault of her twat, leaving half of his thigh gaping open He punched downward into her throat once more and she rolled away from him. Whatever had hold of Wanda's body was some sort of parasite—it needed her alive to exist, at least in a physical sense. The door pulled open behind him and a thin, pock-marked face peeked in. Roy wasted no time pushing his way past the short Hispanic man staring in confusion.

\*\*\*

He could hardly see in the dark hallway beyond the freezer, but the warmth was welcomed in his numb extremities. The wailing stopped him from relishing in the change in temperature. He shoved Juan away and slammed the door shut behind him. He couldn't see Juan's face clearly, but he could read the reaction of his body language at the infant-like crying beyond the door.

"NO!" Roy said.

"The baby?!" Juan answered, trying to force Roy away.

"It's not a baby," Roy answered.

Juan continued to try to pull him away from the door, intent on rescuing the child he thought was freezing to death.

"It's not a fuckin' baby!" Roy said, and punched Juan in the nose.

He ran for it and didn't even stop at the thoughts of the guards; his momentum carried him down the poorly lit hallway and into the main warehouse.

\*\*\*

His body wasn't functioning in stealth mode as he made his way towards the back door exit. His lungs were on the brink of hyperventilation, and his thigh bled a sticky trail down his shin. He nearly lost control of his bowels at the sight of two young men from the crew who beat him unconscious posted as guards beside the exit. They jumped from their seats, both reaching behind their backs, and Roy knew they were about to blow his head clean off his shoulders. He froze as they looked with anger and confusion at the bloodied gringo... And that's when Juan appeared, screaming.

Roy could only decipher what Juan said by his frantic movements; he wanted out of the building at all costs. Juan attempted to push past the two guards, but was stopped. He nearly wept as they looked to each other, well aware of his drunken escapades, curious as to the reason for his terror.

The answer to all their questions came scampering down the hallway on wobbling appendages that were never meant to be manipulated into their present state. The creature walked vagina-first, displaying a disfigured baby face just above a twat gnashing its teeth. Poor Wanda's spine looked as if it might snap in two; Roy had seen women on the internet who weren't even *that* flexible. He shuddered and darted behind the gunmen, who stood in disbelief as the hooker-beast came for them.

***

Roy pushed his way through the exit door, with Juan close behind. Gunshots rang out, followed closely by the screams of grown men. He was in such shock that he couldn't feel his legs. Juan's feet pounded the pavement behind him as they ran around the side of the building.

The parking lot was nearly empty but for the cars of those guarding the warehouse, and those two men, Roy guessed, were probably being eaten alive. He couldn't push himself any farther when he felt a hand on his wrist—Juan was leading him to a black single-cab pickup truck. Roy looked back to see the figure of a woman in the darkness near the building. She stood erect, but unnaturally so.

"HURRY!" he urged Juan, who had his hand in his pants pocket, searching for his keys. "HURRY THE FUCK UP!"

Juan produced a set of keys, thanking God in Spanish, and opened the driver's side door. Roy wasted no time crawling through to the passenger seat, not risking being left behind, when Juan remembered getting punched in the face and left behind to become Wanda's dinner.

"*Pendejo!*" Juan screamed as he fumbled with his keys, and Roy wasn't sure if he was cursing himself or the gringo he'd aided in escaping. He didn't care, he just wanted to survive. Juan could call Roy's mother a filthy whore and he would nod, smile, and wait for the engine to turn over, if Juan could get him safely away from the Wanda-creature.

Empty beer cans littered the floorboard and it smelled like someone had shit in the glove box, but the crappy old truck started right up and Juan navigated toward the street. Roy looked back and, through the tinted window, with his only half-functioning eye, he could see her contorting once more to appear human and then stumbling away.

\*\*\*

Wanda was in there somewhere—the demonic force was in control, but she could still see through her own eyes. She couldn't feel her own legs carrying her out to the sidewalk but she somehow knew where she was headed. The entity that had taken her over could read her memories, and hungrily they made her go to the best place to feed: the truck stop.

# TINY

HE HAD EXITED the freeway and made his way across town. He kept his windows rolled down in an attempt to let the stench of his body odor get carried away on the breeze. Tiny was a regular at the truck stop, and he hoped to make it in time to get a date with his favorite lady: Wanda.

His route kept him in the area, and he liked it that way; there was good food, police who usually minded their own business, and a truck stop providing blow jobs to lonesome men like himself. Tiny glanced into his oversized side mirror and what he saw was one ugly motherfucker, but he knew it wouldn't matter to Wanda. He was nervous about a particular request he had tonight, though; it made him sweat outrageously at the thought of asking her. Last time she'd allowed it, pretended to enjoy it even, and he made a mental note of the date, exactly one month before. His cock stiffened at the thought of burying his face between her thighs, feeling the warmth of her blood on his tongue...the taste of her drove him crazy. Many chose the back door this time of the month, but Tiny had finally gotten up the nerve to ask and she said yes—he earned his red wings. He thought about how his cheeks had sticky clots hanging from them, and his upper lip smelled like unwashed pussy for days. He nearly couldn't contain himself and pressed the gas pedal to the floorboard. The memory of her so soft, slippery, and warm in his mouth caused him to spasm. He nearly lost control of his rig, but the thought of jackknifing into a ditch and dying with a raging hard-on brought him back to his senses. He eased his foot off the pedal, slowing his truck to a safer speed.

"Easy now," he spoke out loud to himself.

His cheeks were hot and sweat began to gather in places he wished it wouldn't. He always worried that the atrocious scent of his nuts might be brought to his attention...again. That's why he needed Wanda so badly; she was never as hurtful as those other women.

That's when his headlights danced across her, walking along the roadside like an answer to his lustful prayers. Tiny would recognize that yellow hair and strut anywhere. He was lucky that he had slowed his rig down already, or he might have blown right past his truck stop angel. He came to a stop in the middle of the empty road.

"Need a ride?" he yelled over to her.

She stopped, and for a moment he worried she might not recognize him in the dark.

\*\*\*

The entity was guiding her back to her place of employment. Her hands moved of their own accord to slide her skirt back down and cover her bare breasts with her shirt. Their voices spoke in her mind, demanded to be fed human flesh. She didn't even notice the headlights, the sound of the truck, but the voice hailing her sparked a memory in her brain, one of oniony body odor. She turned her head and her arm raised involuntarily, her mouth spoke against her will.

"Tiny. Hello."

The sound of her own voice in her ears caused her to panic, but there wasn't a damn thing she could do. She could see herself walking around the side of his truck, passing through his headlights and climbing in. It was like watching some home video she was too fucked up to remember recording.

\*\*\*

The cab light shone down upon her for a few seconds even after she closed the door. She looked pale, and her belly seemed a bit bloated. There was blood on her thighs, running down her legs.

"Are you okay, Wanda?" Tiny asked.

"A little accident," she answered.

She was screaming in her mind, wishing to plead with him to take her to a hospital.

He smiled. "That time of the month?"

"Yes. It is," the thing answered for her.

Her nose caught his scent, and she knew her answer excited him. The demon could see her memories of him and used his weakness for period blood against him.

"Take me to our usual spot and I'll let you help me get cleaned up."

She thought he would surely go into cardiac arrest as his truck leapt forward and he hurried to obtain his reward beneath her skirt.

# LA CURANDERA

JUAN SPED THROUGH a small neighborhood, the sidewalks filled with children after dark. The yards were well-maintained but the houses were older, most looking as if a party was going on. Music thumped with heavy bass in the proximity and the smell of food drifted into the cab of the truck.

"Where are we going?" Roy asked.

Juan never took his eyes off the road, just shook his head. Roy knew he was terrified. Cuervo would want his head for helping Roy.

"Where are we going?"

"Helping you, but no hospital," Juan replied, and pointed to Roy's injury.

Juan was taking him somewhere other than a hospital to seek medical treatment, somewhere Cuervo couldn't find them.

"*Un doctoro?*" Roy attempted to remember his junior high-level Spanish and failed miserably.

Juan laughed. "*Si, gringo. Un doctoro.*" He mimicked Roy.

"Give me a fuckin' break, I'm trying!"

"I speak English, fucker."

"How the fuck would I know that?" Roy asked.

"Just calm down, I'm taking you to *la curandera*, she's like *un doctoro*," Juan said.

"I know a little Spanish, but not a lot." A pain cutting through his leg cut Roy off. "Fuck, hurry!"

"*Mira*, we're here," Juan said.

Juan came to a stop along the sidewalk of one of the only houses without any lights on.

The yard came to life with growling and snarling, and in the light of the full moon Roy could see a dog fighting to free itself from a length of rope fastened to its collar. It was a short-haired mutt of some sort, its breed mixture indistinguishable. All he knew for sure was that it stood at the same height as his dick, and that worried him. The bleeding had tapered off from his wounds, but the open gash looked terrible; it would certainly grow gangrenous if left untreated. Juan went back to the cab of his truck and dug beneath the edge of the seat. He came back carrying a Styrofoam container obviously from leftover takeout. The stench permeating Roy's nostrils reminded him of Jean Claude: it smelled like whatever it used to be had begun to rot, and the rancid odor coupled with his loss of blood caused him to turn his back to Juan and heave onto the street. The dog calmed down, and the sound of it chomping greedily at the chunk of mystery meat Juan offered up got Roy's stomach rolling again.

"What is that?" Roy asked, edging closer to Juan to keep away from the dog, even though it seemed content with the offering dropped by its feet.

"*Tacos de lengua*," Juan whispered.

Roy didn't completely understand Spanish, but he recognized the last word and recalled Hector talking about tacos made from the tongues of cows. If his stomach wasn't empty, he may have barfed again from the smell of the obviously rotten meat. He straightened himself and followed Juan as he made his way to the front door of the house, dropping little mounds of meat along the way to keep the dog satisfied. He rapped on the door and waited, licking the soured grease from his fingers.

There was a flickering beyond the tiny window in the door, a candle. The young woman who answered looked like an angel with beautiful eyes, irises so dark they were nearly black. Her gaze swept over Juan and Roy, pausing on Roy's shredded leg. She motioned them inside and walked ahead of them. Both Juan and Roy's eyes wandered the interior of the house and the fireplace, lined with pictures of the young woman and an older woman. She couldn't have been more than twenty years old, but something in her eyes was much older.

"Take a seat," she said, and Roy eased himself down onto a couch.

They sat on an old leather sofa and awaited the medical attention Roy desperately needed. He examined his open wound and was horrified to see the flesh about the ragged edges had grown black, and in the tiny living room he could smell that it was already infected. His head spun and sweat sprung up on his forehead—a battle to remain conscious was beginning in his brain. He felt the urge to vomit slowly clenching his stomach, and for a moment he grew embarrassed to look like such a pussy in front of the young woman She had disappeared down a dark hallway. Soft light came from the adjacent kitchen, but the room in which they sat was almost black but for the candle the young woman had left on the coffee table at Juan's side. Juan's nervously fidgeting silhouette beside Roy was not a welcoming image. The light played over one side of his face, and began to distort and pull outward. As it wavered it played tricks with Roy's eyes, causing Juan to appear monstrous. The infection was already taking hold of his brain, causing him to hallucinate; that was a really bad sign. Roy closed his eyes and ran his hands over his face. His need to puke multiplied, and he knew it wasn't something he would be able to control. As his mouth began watering and his guts knotted painfully, he leaned forward, waiting for the heaving to commence.

He opened his eyes, and a flash of light nearly blinded him. A light was switched on and his eyes fought to adjust for a moment before he could see in front of him. There stood the young woman, and at her side was an older woman. They appeared to be related by the resemblance in their faces, the same black eyes. The old woman took a glance at Roy's festering leg, then shook her head and stepped back. The young woman gripped her by the arm, and there was a silent exchange between them. Roy could see she wasn't interested in treating him, but the young woman persisted, refusing to let the old woman retreat back to her bedroom. Instead, she gave in and nodded.

"My name is Adriana, and this is my grandmother. She will help you," the young woman said, and offered her hand to Roy.

The embarrassment returned to him, but he knew he wouldn't be able to walk on his own. He placed his clammy hand in hers and allowed her to lead him into a side room—it must've been a garage at one point from the looks of it, but now it had a small bed on one wall and shelves filled with books, candles, and jars of herbs.

He was helped down onto the bed and Juan finally spoke in Spanish to the older woman. She nodded and looked to Roy and began instructing Adriana.

"How bad is it?" he asked.

"Very bad," Adriana answered. "Take off your pants."

Roy hesitated.

"Do you need help?" she asked.

He began unbuttoning his jeans, and she sat beside him. His hands shook as she assisted him in pulling his pants off. He cried out, embarrassment filled him; he didn't want her staring at the not-so-impressive bulge of his flaccid dick. The old woman came over to examine him and crossed herself. He knew then that he was in really bad shape.

"If this is out of your hands, I can just go to the hospital," he said, his teeth beginning to chatter and his body growing cold.

"No doctor can fix this infection," Adriana said, her voice completely serious.

"This came from evil, the devil himself or one of his servants."

Roy thought about Wanda, the creature she had become, and he knew what Adriana said was true.

"This takes a different kind of doctor. Luckily for you, white boy, my grandmother knows the old ways."

"What can she do?" he asked as his body continued to convulse.

"She will take out the evil and your leg will heal," Adriana answered.

"What is she, a witch or something?"

"*La Curandera*," Adriana answered. "She is the only thing that will save you. Keep quiet now and let her work."

\*\*\*

Roy's leg had festered to the point of splitting. It seeped a slimy fluid and reeked like a septic tank. He was stretched out on the bed, shaking and dripping with sweat. The old woman stood over him, clutching an egg in her right hand. Adriana wafted sage smoke over him from a lit bundle in her hand; it crawled over his body and up his nose in the tight confines of the small space. The *curandera* began chanting a prayer over him—his heart seized in his chest. She began rubbing the egg over Roy's skin as she continued to pray—blisters rose on his skin in response to her ministrations. Roy gritted his teeth in agony as his whole body began to burn. The chanting intensified as she ran the egg over his leg. The gaping hole there ran pus like a yellow river down onto the mattress beneath him. She called for Adriana to light a white candle on a table at his bedside, then poured water into a crystal glass waiting there and cracked the tainted egg into it. Roy could see the concern in her face before he even got a look at the glass. Adriana paused as she began to return to smudging, staring into the water. Floating in it was not the golden yolk of an ordinary egg, but a thick black blood clot, and trapped in its coagulated chunks was a deformed chick. It twitched in the glass as its darkness seeped down into the clear water, consuming it. The old witch threw a handful of salt into the glass, and the chick erupted into a mass of writhing maggots. Roy looked to Adriana, his eyes begging for answers as the old woman spoke.

"What is she saying?"

"She says we need to go to the source and kill it there, before it..."

"Before it what?"

"Takes your whole body," Adriana answered.

# RED WINGS AND TEETH

TINY PULLED HIS truck into the gravel lot beside the truck stop and looked over to Wanda, who sat quietly smiling at him. He nodded his head back to his sleeper and she giggled. She seemed more inviting than she usually was, and it excited him to no end. She leapt between the seats and began clearing the small bunk of its usual junk.

"Take off your clothes," she said.

He stumbled over himself and fell across her on the small bed.

"Sorry, Wanda," he said, as she rolled him over.

His cock stiffened as she began freeing him of his clothing. She was strong and her need seemed urgent, almost as if she really wanted him. He allowed himself to believe in the fantasy. He hesitated to remove his stained t-shirt, but she yanked it over his head. The darkness of the sleeper eased his self-consciousness; he never liked being fully nude in front of women because of his weight and his skin condition. The smell of him permeated the tight enclosure, but she didn't seem to notice. She now stripped off her own shirt, and her perky breasts bounced as she knelt over him.

"What would you like tonight?" she asked, her voice filled with longing.

He knew he had to say it, though he almost couldn't bring himself to, but she had suggested it when he first picked her up, so he blurted it out.

"A blow job and..." he said.

"And?"

"Red wings," he mumbled.

"You got it," she said.

She peeled his underwear down and his dick sprang out, standing at attention. He could smell blood; it excited him like nothing he had ever experienced. He moaned as she licked his shaft and began teasing the head of his cock with the tip of her tongue. He had never paid for something so wonderful in all his life; usually it was quick and over with in less than ten minutes. He felt his wad building up; she would get a gut full when he came. That was the other thing he always appreciated about

Wanda: she was a swallower. She slid her mouth down over his dick and began bobbing away. His toes curled, and he got brazen enough to place his chubby hand on the back of her head. He tangled his stubby fingers in her stringy hair and enjoyed the feeling of her hot wet mouth sliding over him. He was impressed with her deep-throat action, though he knew his package probably wasn't near as big as other men she was accustomed to sucking off. She cupped his balls in one hand, massaged them a bit, and he could hold himself back no longer. He came in hot spasms and he felt her ease her mouth free, but she sucked every drop of his cum like an oniony milkshake. He was breathing heavily and sweating like a hog.

"My turn," she said into the darkness of the sleeper, and the eagerness in her voice stiffened him all over again. Tiny wondered, if she enjoyed his tongue job, then maybe she'd let him fuck her bloody twat as well. She lay back. He got on his knees and crawled up between her legs Her skirt was still pulled down, but he decided to act out his sexual fantasies of teasing and pleasing a woman. He decided to start by lapping up the dried blood at her calves first. He lowered his mouth and greedily sucked at the irony clots. He could feel her reaction, he knew her anticipation would build the higher up her leg he licked, and he hoped once he finally reached her gash she would be screaming. Maybe, just once in his life, he could feel an honest to goodness orgasm out of a woman. He hadn't anticipated the amount of blood she had shed, and he felt sorry for her to have had such an embarrassing mishap with her monthly cycle. He wanted to be extra good for her, to take away her troubles, if only for a moment. He slid his tongue around like a fat grub worm, working his way up each leg, licking up every drop of spilled blood. He was at her milky thighs when his eagerness got the best of him. He ran his hand up her skirt, seeking a warm, wet hole. His fingers fumbled over something jagged and she giggled. He paused... She hadn't giggled at all, but her pussy had.

His fingers slid into what felt like a bear trap, his flesh caught in a serrated vice. He tried to pull himself free, but only felt his meat being torn, his fingers snapping. He hollered and felt his own warm blood run down his arm. She sat forward, gripping his shoulders, pulling him into her further. His cries would be obvious to a passerby. He was not in ecstasy, but excruciating pain, so she tore his windpipe clean out of his throat with her right hand. Blood rained across her face, and she grinned into the darkness. Her left hand grazed something bulbous on his back, and a disgusted familiarity registered in the human side of her subconscious. He wasn't quite dead when she pinched and mashed the giant boil between her fingers. Pus came out like a yellow fountain and with satisfaction her vagina fed as she milked him of every ounce of the vile smelling liquid. Her twat maw released his hand, and she ended him completely by driving his face directly into it, his flabby cheeks turned to nothing more than hamburger meat. She focused her attention on emptying every boil on his body while the demonic monster housed within her private parts dined upon Tiny's stinking corpse.

# SKINNING A WHITE RAT

WANDA CLIMBED FROM the truck with a bloated gut. The demons had grown tired of the taste of Tiny's meat and abandoned him naked and dead within his sleeper. The urge to empty her bowels was intense, and for a moment the entities instructed her to cop a squat and squeeze out a massive steamer in the gravel, but they knew it would only draw attention to their host. Rifling through her collected memories informed it that the truck stop restroom would be the place to relieve her body of its gorge.

She was still hidden away somewhere in her mind, but diminishing slowly; soon Wanda would be completely lost. She knew their intent and she was helpless to stop them. She read them as they read her, and found glimpses of a world of complete darkness and pain. It had found a gateway into the land of the living, that portal being her overly-used vagina, opened by her regret and the blood of a rooster named Jean Claude Van Damme. She knew that by nightfall she would fade away, her body would be cast aside, and the flesh-hungry beasts would be freed upon the earth. She wanted to fight back, but didn't see any possible way she could.

The red wedge-heeled shoes she'd chosen that morning were easy to walk in for Wanda, but the entity swarming within her found them cumbersome and waddled on the sides of her feet towards the truck stop restroom.

"Where the hell have you been?"

She ignored the voice and kept on her path to relieve herself of what felt like thirty pounds of shit in her gut.

"Don't ignore me!"

She fell forward after a sudden sucker punch to the back of her head. Rolling over in the dark, she could see a familiar face illuminated for a split second by a cigarette lighter. A red glow danced before his white face, the lit end of a cheap cigar. The beasts felt a swell of anger from Wanda, and her memories became open to them.

"You were supposed to be here hours ago."

His fists were still clinched at the ends of his lanky arms. He was not a big man, but his body had the natural muscle tone of a predatory animal, feral and dangerous. The night had already claimed the sky, and there weren't any lights at the outermost edges of the parking lot, so his eyes squinted to study her silhouette.

"Got sick. Started my rag," the demons said with Wanda's voice.

His fist came fast and hard across her chin and he stood over her in a silent rage. He was done talking, and he didn't want to hear any excuses.

"Get cleaned up and get to work. Tonight I take one hundred percent, bitch," he said, and strutted away like some puffed up mini-rooster.

Wanda grinned, though Jim never saw it. The entities couldn't wait to taste his pale flesh; the darkness beneath his albino hide would taste divine. If it weren't for the need to empty her bowels, they would have skinned him like a white man-banana right then, but the need for secrecy was far too great...at least until midnight.

***

Only twenty-four hours earlier, Wanda was hovering over the truck stop commode, expelling a demon of a different variety. This time when she pulled up her skirt, she decorated the toilet with a stream of meaty chunks of Hector and Tiny, splattering down onto the yellowed porcelain like a shower of raw sewage. Wanda didn't even bother locking the door; her body needed to be emptied before the gluttonous spirits could gorge themselves once more. Their target was placed on the skinny albino pimp who could have been mistaken for a low-rent Johnny Winter. He went by the name of Jim Dandy, yet he never came to the rescue of anyone—instead, he had a knack for leading young women down a path of abuse. Wanda wanted to see him suffer; she couldn't deny that finally having the power to hurt him gave her an ounce of satisfaction. She was preparing herself to die, and the only thing she asked of the entity controlling her was that it would kill Jim Dandy, that it would skin him alive. Her murderous thoughts pleased the beasts writhing inside of her like ethereal worms, and they agreed to appease her. A void in her gut growled hungrily. She never wiped her ass, simply pulled her skirt down and walked over to the floor-length strip of polished stainless-steel that doubled as a mirror. The demon admired the ravenous shell it now inhabited; she was desirable, which meant she could be used to lure foolish men to their deaths. At the midnight hour, her body would become its property forever.

"What the fuck are you doing?" His voice echoed in the single-shitter restroom.

Her gaze caught Jim's reflection through the etched-in phone numbers and obscenities. She smiled, and the demons smiled with her.

"What a fuckin' mess! Did you shit yourself?"

"Fuck you," Wanda answered.

He stepped into the restroom, sliding the door closed behind him. "I'm gonna make you lick that toilet clean."

She turned to face him as he strutted toward her. The sole of his snakeskin boot slipped in a pool of liquid shit winding its way toward a floor drain in the grout of the tile. Jim's tough-ass expression fled his face in favor of surprise as he fell backwards onto the filth-stained floor. The demons controlled her body as Wanda pounced onto his chest. Jim brought his hand up in a callused fist against her eye. It rocked her head back, but she recovered and stared down at him, seemingly unfazed. He awkwardly attempted to strike her again, only to have his fist caught in her palm. Wanda rolled his wrist backwards in a sharp violent motion, snapping his bones. The shock on his face was worth being possessed, as it filled Wanda with triumphant glee. Her skirt rode up, displaying the twisted baby-like face above her twat; it snapped its hideous maw at Jim as he tried to fight. He opened his mouth to scream, but it was muffled as she crammed her other fist into his throat. His cries were nothing but whimpering gurgles as she crammed it further, loosening his bottom jaw with a wet cracking sound before completely unhinging it with a forceful thrust of her arm. Jim's eyes bulged and became red with broken blood vessels as he suffocated. He writhed a bit, but it wasn't enough to shake the whore from his chest, and he died with the scent of Wanda's shit in his nostrils. She slid around over his face to snake her arm down his throat until her hand could go no further. When the Wanda-creature gripped a handful of his slippery insides, the lost human inside thought it felt vaguely like pulling the insides out of a jack-o'-lantern. Yellow light filled the restroom as the door came open; Wanda was nearly shoulder deep in her former pimp when she heard the cursing of an elderly Hispanic woman from behind her. Those hitchhiking in her skin shuddered at the words, and for the first time Wanda could feel them panic.

# THE EXORCISM

Roy knew where Wanda worked; she was his neighbor and former friend. He never had a problem with her until she asked to borrow his Ouija board. He'd wanted to refuse her, but the grief in her drunken eyes swayed his heart. He'd never guessed that she would kill his rooster and get herself possessed in the process. It all felt so unreal.

The *curandera* threw the truck stop restroom door open, and Roy nearly collapsed at the scene in front of him. Juan stood back in shock as Wanda slid her arm free of Jim Dandy's gaping jaws, dragging a long bloody handful of insides out onto the floor, then looked back over her shoulder. The old woman went to war with the creature, throwing holy water and chanting. Wanda screeched, then leapt up onto the back of the shit-covered toilet, perching there for only a second before scrambling up the wall. It defied gravity, but it didn't surprise Adriana or her grandmother. They rushed inside the tight restroom, wielding handfuls of salt and vials of consecrated oils. Juan pushed Roy in, but refused to step inside himself.

"Lock it!" Adriana screamed as Wanda looked to the door in desperation.

Roy acted quickly, flinging his body against the only exit and twisting the latch. Wanda jumped onto his back, sinking her teeth into his neck. Roy could feel the venomous teeth of her crotch ripping at his t-shirt. He grabbed her by a fistful of her hair and pried her snapping fangs off of him before flipping her over his shoulder onto the bathroom floor. The old woman moved swiftly, emptying a small bag tied to her belt into her palm and throwing the contents into Wanda's face. The possessed whore screamed, her face blistering instantly, and her eyes rolled back. The *curandera*'s words seemed familiar to Roy, a prayer. He watched as Wanda dragged herself backwards, attempting to hide in the tight space behind the filthy toilet. Adriana repeated her grandmother's words; their intensity grew into a fierce chant. As Wanda spat and cussed at them in English, they prayed in Spanish and doused her with holy water.

Roy had always thought those old movies about exorcisms were hokey until he witnessed it firsthand. With every one of his senses he experienced the fight for the soul of a wretched woman, a sinner who'd unwittingly opened herself to the powers of the darkness. His leg pulsed each time the consecrated water burned into Wanda's flesh, and his wound seeped yellow pus. Pressure built beneath his skin until he, too, writhed in agony and prayed the demons would release them both. The smell of the slovenly shitter grew more putrid with the stink of loosed bodily fluids and singed flesh. Wanda spoke a mixture of English and what Roy guessed to be Latin as the beasts inside of her challenged the old shaman woman. Her limbs twisted until he was certain every joint in her body was broken beyond repair. A wailing issued forth from the demonic twat between her legs.

"She is me and I am she. I will take him too. There's nothing you can do!"

"Callate!" the curandera yelled.

"She will cut you out like a cancer," Adriana said as she doused Wanda once more with holy water.

Roy felt pressure building in his wound again; it bulged with festering rotted tissue like a putrid balloon. He gripped his thigh and screamed. The old woman turned to him and emptied a vial on the bloated mass; it popped, sending a shower of discharge flying to the ceiling. The pain was an agony that he had never felt before, like a burst of flames consuming his flesh down to the bone. Roy held his hands up, begging for mercy, as Adriana pulled another bottle from a satchel she wore. She showered him with it again. It seared into his skin like a rain of battery acid, and yet he was thankful. He didn't want to end up like Wanda, a soulless monster with a cock-demon.

Wanda laughed with the voice of a chorus of chain smokers as the face between her legs giggled in a high-pitched childlike tone.

"The hour draws nigh, old woman. This woman will be mine...and soon, so will Roy," the beast said.

It crawled over to the corpse of Jim Dandy and jammed its thumbs into his eye sockets. It removed his pink eyes and held them out to the holy women before slurping them off the ends of its thumbnails like a child stealing black olives from a salad bar. It chewed them up and swallowed them with an exaggerated gulp, then pointed to Roy as he stared in terror.

"I bet his eyes taste much better."

Adriana looked to her grandmother. The old woman understood enough English to know the demons were basically declaring victory. The *curandera* nodded her head solemnly. Adriana reached into the satchel and removed something enfolded in black velvet. The old woman kissed the object reverently, then removed it from its protective wrapping. She cradled the crucifix carved of dark wood in her wrinkled palms and turned back to face her foe. As she lifted the holy relic, the triumph in the possessed woman's face faded away, and her monstrous twat hissed. Wanda scurried away on her hands and knees, slipping and sliding through the pools of diarrhea. She fell against the toilet, breaking her nose on the porcelain bowl. Blood spurted down her lips and dripped from her chin down onto her chest.

Roy could feel that his wound was tainted; the putrid poison in his blood was spreading, and his stomach soured as a cold sweat dampened his skin. Adriana came to his side as her grandmother fearlessly continued to wage war with the evil they had trapped in the truck stop ladies room. Roy was beginning to convulse, and Adriana knew it was not only a sickness of the body, but of the spirit as well. If her grandmother didn't end it soon, both Roy and Wanda would be lost.

"The whore opened the doorway. The Lord of Pandemonium sees you. He's coming. He wants you, black eyes!" Wanda growled.

She lashed out feebly as the crucifix was pressed against her forehead. The *curandera*'s voice did not falter as she continued her prayers, hoping to release the haggard prostitute from the devil's bondage. The screeching of an infant filled the tiny space, echoing off the tile walls. Roy closed his eyes as his body seized up; he could feel his heart thumping painfully. A cold wind stole his breath as a cacophony of inhuman voices screamed. Roy cracked one eye open just enough to see a black void had opened, with unearthly gales wailing out at them. Black wisps of smoky tentacles were pouring from Wanda's mouth and vagina, retreating into the dark beyond the human world and slithering back into their true home. The old woman stood up against the winds, holding the crucifix out before her. It wasn't until the wormhole to Hell closed that she began to tremble. Roy felt the agony in his body abating, slowly ebbing away as relief replaced it.

\*\*\*

Adriana helped Roy to his feet. He surveyed the restroom: Wanda was either unconscious or dead, and the stinky corpse of the albino pimp lay in a pool of shit with a dislocated bottom jaw and no eyes. Juan beat the door until they let him in.

"What the hell are we going to do with them?" Roy asked.

Juan whispered to Adriana and her grandmother, and they seemed to come to a hushed agreement before answering him.

"There is only one person who can make this all go away, but it will cost us," Adriana answered.

"I have a good savings built up, it's yours. You and your grandmother earned it," Roy answered.

"She's not talking about money, gringo," Juan said.

The old woman shuffled past them. The mighty glamour she had once wrapped about her, making her seem so powerful, had gone, and her age was dreadfully apparent.

"*Llama al Chamuco y El Gusano,*" she told her grandchild in resignation.

As she exited the truck stop ladies room, the old woman brought a handkerchief to her mouth to cough. The yellow parking lot lights backlit the thin material, and Roy was certain he could see blood spatter into the folds of the white linen. He couldn't believe the name she had spoken; he was a legend among the seedy underground, and it turned Roy's skin cold.

"You're not calling El Gusano, are you? He's Chamuco's right-hand man."

"We don't have a choice," Adriana answered.

"But you work for Cuervo, Chamuco's rival and apparent enemy," he said to Juan, who was obviously frightened at the mention of the soup man, but had suggested it as a last option.

"I was there when Hector got killed. What if he blames me, or thinks I helped Cuervo kill him?" Roy added.

"We're not sure he even knows about Hector yet," Juan said.

"Anyone left in the freezer, or stupid enough to open it, don't work for Cuervo anymore, and an enemy of your enemy is your friend," Adriana said.

"I just don't want to be a part of that world. I don't want to end up in jail or dead," Roy said.

"What choice do you have? If we wait too long, the *chorizo* is gonna be called and then we're all fucked," Juan said.

"You're already a part of this," Adriana said.

Roy's gut knotted, he knew she was right. He looked back at the bathroom door as a chill ran over him. If Juan hadn't opened the freezer, Roy's body would have never been recovered. He would have been shit out by Wanda by now. And if not, Cuervo would have killed him. He was a dead man walking already. He was no longer under the protection of Hector, and Cuervo would have him killed for escaping the freezer. Roy only hoped that since Cuervo tried to kill him, it would play in his favor in the eyes of Chamuco, and that his own reputation of producing the best fighting roosters in the southwest would save his ass.

"Hector told me maybe Chamuco would hire me for some other jobs, besides cockfighting, but I don't know if the offer still stands. What if it doesn't?"

"At least you had an offer," Juan said.

"Maybe I could trade him some of my best roosters?" Roy offered in desperation.

"He's gonna demand more than roosters," Juan said.

# THE SOUP MAN

THE OWNER OF the truck stop knew better than to interfere when he saw the black hearse drive into his parking lot. He kept his ass inside the convenience store, and pretended not to notice when the driver stepped out dressed in a black suit. El Gusano wasn't often called to leave the barn of death, but when he was he made sure to leave a lasting impression on all who laid eyes on him. He wore black boots, the toes tipped in shining silver, much like the boots that had nearly left Roy blind in the back freezer of El Cuervo's *carniceria*. Roy avoided making eye contact as El Gusano spoke softly in Spanish to Adriana and her grandmother. Instead, his eyes fell on the soup man's belt buckle. It was a ram's head carved of silver. He had heard through the grapevine that El Chamuco dabbled in *magia negra*, black magic—the left hand of *brujeria*...Satanism. Roy shivered as he eavesdropped, understanding almost nothing, but what he did decipher was that Wanda didn't make it and she, too, would go into the soup barrels. As for the guy she was dismembering when they found her, the soup man wanted him for other reasons. Roy had no idea what they were, but it made the old woman frown in disgust.

"*Oigan, pendejos,*" the soup man said, and eyed Roy and Juan.

Roy still didn't take his eyes from the ram's head belt buckle. He felt that death was very near, and any wrong move would find him thrown into a steel drum.

"Hey, white boy. Look at my face, not my dick!"

Roy looked into his eyes. The dark bags beneath them spoke of a sleepless man, if he could call himself a man anymore. His gaze felt more like that of a feral animal, leery and dangerous.

"Yes, I speak English, *pendejos*. I know many, many things, things you wish to keep secret."

"I—I'm sorry, I didn't..."

"*Callate y escucha.*"

"He said shut up and listen," Juan whispered to Roy.

Adriana and her grandmother stood silent, their eyes fixed on Roy and Juan.

"You have a choice to make. You can either die like the old crow you worked for, Cuervo." El Gusano rolled up his sleeve, revealing an arm covered in tattoos, and pointed at one just above his wrist, the Baphomet.

"Or you can serve something that never dies, that's what Chamuco offers you."

Juan nodded before quickly offering his allegiance to a new cartel. He glanced over at Roy, who stood quietly, thinking. Adriana was correct: El Cuervo wanted Roy dead anyway, and he knew he couldn't face down Chamuco and the soup man on his own. It was better to join them than try to fight them.

"You'll be two sets of eyes and ears, *ratas a mi servicio*."

"*No soy un soplon, jefe*," Juan said respectfully.

"*Si, tu lo eres*," Gusano answered with a grin as he gripped the pistol sticking out of his jeans. Juan nodded, understanding the silent threat.

"I will take your offer," Roy answered.

"We'll be in touch." El Gusano smiled, his front teeth crooked and sharp, the maw of a beast hidden in the scabby skin of a man.

The *curandera* remained silent, her eyes searching the soup man. Roy couldn't help but wonder if what he was seeing in her eyes was regret.

"Chamuco will be calling for you soon." He winked at Adriana before going to work making Wanda and Jim disappear.

# MAGIA NEGRA

EL CHAMUCO STOOD naked in the light of the moon; the power of its illumination penetrated his skin all the way to his bones. He did not want to be an ordinary man; he wanted to be more than that. He wanted to be a god. El Gusano lingered behind him, preparing to grant his deepest desires. They stood in the bone field, the field of death beside the old barn, while the Gusanas pulled bodies free of the earth by the wire wrapped around their necks. They sang while they harvested corpses with fatty tissue still clinging to their bones. El Gusano studied his employer; the money Chamuco provided would have impressed many people, but to the *brujo* and his siblings it was nothing compared to their lust for death and chaos. Their dream was to see Pandemonium reign.

The cartel leader demanded they perform a powerful ritual to finally crush his rival, since Cuervo was now aware of Chamuco's intent. They were fully prepared to grant his wish, they just didn't know if he realized what exactly he was asking for. The twin *brujas* returned, dragging a bloated corpse behind them. Its stink stirred up a band of coyotes not far away in the deserts beyond the barn. The women laughed and smiled toothless grins as they approached the drug lord known for his stone cold behavior. His eyes fell on the remains and a slight tremor betrayed that he wasn't as hardcore as he liked people to believe. The *brujo* laughed alongside his sisters, then slapped Chamuco on the shoulder before leading him back into the barn.

***

The skin slid easily from the corpse, like the peel off an overripe fruit. Juices dripped, flowing down over the *brujo's* hands and snaking along to his elbows before dropping to the floor at his bare feet. Chamuco swallowed the gorge burning the back of his throat as they anointed his body with the vile putrefying fat of the dead man. He needed this to finally overthrow El Cuervo. The sisters led him before an altar of bones, both human and animal, illuminated by the glow of black candles. El

Gusano began a prayer to the dark ones—*los siete espiritus intranquilos*, the seven restless sprints, a conduit to commune with the devil himself. He sought to commune with *El Hombre Sombra*. The *brujo* filled his mouth with alcohol, then blew it into Chamuco's face, blinding the cartel leader for a moment. When he opened his eyes, the flames atop the candles leapt high into the air. The maggot sisters stripped nude, their flesh marred with stretch marks, stomachs bloated, skin glistening with sweat, as they began to house the spirits of darkness. Their voices came out in harsh growls as they told him of the price he would have to pay for the power he sought. His shadow would control him after sunset and he would have to swallow souls to keep the master appeased. By day, Chamuco would be the most powerful man in his territory, crushing El Cuervo and his men, but after dark he would become a slave to the night, a vessel for *Hombre Sombra*.

He trembled as shadows pulled themselves off the walls and crawled up his legs. He never spoke his acquiescence, but he knew this deal with the lord below was sealed in blood when he sheltered the *Tres Gusanos* and made a pact with them. The witch with warty lips crawled forward as the shadows crept down his throat to whisper the identity of the first soul *Hombre Sombra* demanded: a young *curandera* with black eyes, Adriana. Chamuco would be drawn to her. His reemergence was nigh, and his companion was already in their grasp. Their master would be so pleased.

*Los Tres Gusanos* watched Chamuco flee the barn, his body transforming painfully as he became part of the darkness. It was the first step to fulfilling their vows to the Shadow Man. They would celebrate their success by dining on what El Gusano saved from the corpses of the prostitute and her pimp. Coyotes yelped in the distance as a predator much older than them came into the world of the living once more.

# THE PAST RETURNS

ADRIANA COULD HEAR her grandmother in her bedroom. The old woman was tossing in her sleep and speaking to ghosts from a time long before her granddaughter lived. The young woman listened intently through the thin door as the old woman waged war in her dreams with who she always referred to as *El Hombre Sombra*, the Shadow Man. Her grandmother had told Adriana of her battle with him down in her hometown when she was young, and once revealed some the scars from the fight with him. They were puckered and pink many decades after being inflicted upon her. She shuddered when she showed a few of them to her granddaughter, and even at a young age Adriana knew her grandmother's mental scars ran deeper than those in her flesh.

Her grandmother said the Shadow Man always attached himself to men who craved control and turned them into monsters. He took pleasure in creating chaos and suffering; she had witnessed it with her own eyes. His ultimate goal was to unleash Hell on Earth. He'd nearly succeeded, but the young *curandera* had stopped him. It was a battle her grandmother nearly lost. A lesson she always tried to instill in her grandchild was to beware the lust for power, for it breathes life into unimaginable monsters, beings that could claim the flesh of men and use them as their vehicles of destruction.

\*\*\*

Adriana stepped out into her yard. Her dog whined as it lifted its head to watch her go. The neighborhood was alive with music and children laughing, but beyond their little community stretched the city of Apache Wells in all of its bordertown glory. The same *carniceria* selling a mother her beef for dinner also housed freezers of torture and dealt out kilos of cocaine from the backdoor. The cops were crooked and under the thumb of Cuervo, and surrounding the city were miles of lonesome desert, essentially cutting it off from the rest of the world. Rarely did people pass through, and even rarer did locals leave there alive. Apache Wells was a deserted island along the border, a jewel ready to be claimed by lawless men. Despite all the ugliness, she and her grandmother still refused to find any other place to call home.

Adriana locked the front door behind her and readied herself for the night shift at the convenience store where she worked. Her grandmother didn't make much as a *bruja*. Her services were sought out by quite a few, but the old woman's conscience usually kept her from charging for her services—even the gringo Roy, she didn't accept a penny for saving his life.

She made her way down the dark sidewalk and across the street as the moon loomed low over her. It was one of those nights where Adriana felt like the great yellow orb was following her everywhere she went, stalking her silently. She couldn't help but wonder what the people of the city were doing, if they knew about the darkness hiding within so many souls; if they were aware of the things the night hid, or the things people kept deeply guarded in their own souls, like the woman in the truck stop restroom. She dashed the thought away before the memory of watching the exorcism could send her running back home to the safety she felt just being near her grandmother. She shook her head at the sounds of a woman screaming at her husband; after growing up in such a place, she knew they were all blind to it until they fell victim to it, just as Roy had. Her grandmother told her many stories of things most people would never believe, but the truth in her eyes told Adriana she wasn't lying. After all that she had witnessed herself, she knew evil was real, and it waited just beyond the shadows for everyone.

She hadn't heard from Roy since saving his life, but she knew his reputation. He was the keeper of prized fighters, the man who brought victory and fortune to many men in the cartels. She wasn't naïve enough to hope he would change. She knew the power money held over all men. Roy would be no different, especially after the offer he received from Chamuco. It was one he couldn't turn down unless he wanted to take a ride with Gusano, the soup man, and never return.

\*\*\*

Headlights startled her, but what really set her nerves on edge was when the truck they belonged to began slowing down. She didn't look in its direction until a voice hailed her.

"Hey, little lady. I have a question for you."

Adriana didn't respond; she just walked faster ahead. She was only a few blocks away from the convenience store, and her boss, Alvaro, would tell the guy to get lost. She just had to keep walking.

"Hey, honey. Can you please give me a hand? Please? I'm lost."

The guy was now matching her pace. Alarms went off in her head, and her feet responded. Adriana took off running, but she could hear the truck accelerate. He swerved and nearly hit her. She tried to stop and turn back around, but tripped over a crack in the sidewalk and hit the ground hard, her head bouncing off it. Her vision swam as the sound of his truck door creaking open filled her with terror. Hands gripped her shoulders and yanked her roughly to stand.

"You just had to make things difficult for old Dale, didn't ya?"

A fist struck her in the mouth and everything went dark.

Adriana opened her eyes to see the nighttime desert passing by the truck window.

"Hey, sleeping beauty. I thought you wouldn't wake up," the old man said.

He was old but stout, and had pockmarked skin. His teeth and hair were no longer white but yellow, like piss in snow, from smoking too many cigarettes. His breath reeked of an ashtray, she could smell it from across the truck, and the look in his eyes told her he meant to do horrible things to her. "I'm glad you did, though, it's funner when they're alive and kicking."

Adriana gripped the door handle and pulled, but it wouldn't open. In the silhouette of the cacti and bushes she saw a man standing on the roadside, a drifter with long hair. She beat the window and screamed, but they passed by quickly as her abductor sped up. The truck bounced over the rough dirt road and she turned to fight back, but was met with a hard punch to the face. She fell against the cold window and wept.

"Now, now, this will be over soon," he promised, and she worried how definite his words were.

Adriana felt as if she was going to die. She would be tortured until the end and cast out into the desert for the coyotes and vultures to eat. Her only company would be the worms gathering in her mouth to hear the silent whispers of her spirit as it lamented her final moments at the hands of a predator.

They traveled far into the desert, and while she was weeping and desperately looking for any escape, he just kept laughing, cackling like a hyena, heartless and cruel. He finally brought the truck to a stop and climbed over onto her. The last of her hope slipped away as he groped her roughly and promised to defile her even after death. She couldn't believe how strong he was—even as she fought with all her strength, he still managed to hold her down.

"NO!" she screamed, but her voice sounded distant in her ears.

His hand found her throat, and his grip brought agony to her body and mind. She couldn't breathe, she couldn't scream, and bursts of bright white stars filled her vision. She was slipping away, her ears felt muffled and her chest burned...then suddenly he released her.

Adriana sat up, gasping, and saw that the driver's side window was shattered. The shadow of a man, vaguely familiar, was reaching into the window and gripping Dale by his hair. It was the drifter she had seen for a split second on the road. He must have seen her beating the window and followed the truck deep into the desert. A rush of relief flooded her and tears ran from her eyes. She wept as the drifter yanked Dale's head back, but then she noticed his fingers were glowing like white-hot branding irons, and a new fear flourished in her heart.

*** 

Adriana's grandmother, Consuelo, climbed from her bed. Her body trembled: not with age, but with fear. The voice of the soup man taunted her in her dreams and transformed into a whispering from her past. She knew asking him to take care of the corpses in the truck stop restroom was a mistake as soon as she laid eyes on him. She'd had no idea that he didn't only serve Chamuco, but was in league with the Shadow Man as well. Her dreams hadn't been visited by *Hombre Sombra* in decades, not since she was Adriana's age. But he had found her, and she knew he wouldn't rest until he made her pay. She went to a wooden cabinet and opened a box inside; wrapped in a soft velvet cloth was her only salvation. A pain shot through her chest, stealing her breath, and in her mind she could see her granddaughter swallowed in shadows.

# CARRION

ADRIANA WATCHED AS the man forced his thumbs into Dale's eye sockets. She was never sure if that really was the old man's name, but figured since he meant to kill her, he probably didn't bother concealing his identity. Blood traced the wrinkles in his face, and his mouth hung open in strangled agony. The drifter's thumbs became white-hot as they plunged deeper into the old man's orbital holes; the stench of cooking flesh filled the cab of the truck.

She slid against the passenger side door, unable to open it. Adriana held her hand over her mouth and watched as Dale's skull lit from the inside like a jack-o'-lantern. She felt nothing for the old man; he had been in the process of forcing himself on her before the hitchhiker came out of the dark desert. She feared the smile on the drifter's face, a grin that said he'd like to force his thumbs into her eyes as well.

The old bastard was a predator and had rigged the door so that once Adriana got in, she wouldn't be getting out, and now her only escape was blocked by Dale's corpse. She watched as his flesh blackened and split like an overcooked hot dog. The drifter pulled his face closer to Dale's, then pried his mouth open; a thin stream of white smoke crawled from Dale's charred lips, and the hitchhiker inhaled it. He drew it in and held it deep in his lungs, then leaned against the truck door and sighed, but nothing escaped his mouth. Adriana sat still, heart pounding. She didn't believe she was lucky enough to have escaped his attention, and right at that moment he focused it on her.

His eyes were dark, stubble lined his chin, and he had long dark hair. Adriana would've considered him handsome if it weren't for the cold look on his face. He hadn't spoken a word in his attack on Dale; he'd simply reached into the open window and began roasting Dale's brains from the inside. Adriana thought at first that he had come to rescue her, but the way his eyes roved over her half-naked body before lighting up Dale's skull made her guess otherwise.

"Do I scare you?" he asked.

She didn't answer, not knowing what to say.

He pulled the truck door open before grabbing Dale by the shoulder. The old man's hands were rigidly gripping the steering wheel. The drifter pried them free with little effort, then tossed the corpse out into the dirt. He crawled into the cab of the truck beside her.

"Did I scare you, Adriana?" he asked. "Shall I ask you in your mother's tongue, even though I know I don't have to? *Tienes miedo?*"

"No," she lied.

He leaned forward to retrieve her torn panties from the floorboard of the truck, and held them out to her. Adriana didn't realize how close Dale had come to raping her. She hesitated as he slid closer and pulled her feet into them. The stranger eased them up her legs and over her thighs. She grabbed them, yanking them up quickly, but his hands lingered.

"*Tienes miedo*, Adriana?" he said.

She was shaking. The lingering scent of charred eyes and flesh left her nauseated.

"No," Adriana answered.

"That's a lie," he said, crawling over her.

"No, it's not. Leave me alone," she said.

"I can hear your heart." He laid his head on her chest. "It doesn't sound very brave to me."

Adriana's anxiety made her feel as if Dale's hands were on her throat once more, strangling the breath right out of her.

"There's no need to be afraid," he whispered. "I have other plans for you."

He put his mouth over hers, and her eyes rolled back into her skull. He kissed her and her breath returned, but it was caustic, leaving her mouth tasting like ashes. Her lungs burned, and she coughed.

He released her, then climbed out of the truck. She tried the passenger door once more before resorting to cautiously crawling out the same way he had gone, only to fall to her knees in the powdery desert dirt. Dale's corpse lay only feet away, and the stranger was nowhere to be seen, but she still felt him there.

"Look on him, Adriana." The stranger's voice echoed off the palo verde trees and creosote bushes.

She looked to the dead man as a cold wind swept across the bare skin of her chest; it still ached from his rough hands. A pain tore through her heart. Her hands shook as she attempted to button her torn blouse. She was unsuccessful, so she held it closed, and tears ran down her battered cheeks.

"He would've left you to become carrion; now he is a feast for the night."

Her body trembled as an agonizing cramping twisted her stomach. She fell forward, her hands gripping fistfuls of earth. The stranger appeared from the darkness, his ragged clothing now shed. The white light of the moon was shining brightly, but his entire body moved with shadow. Her pain was too intense to allow her to run; it came in burning waves through every muscle in her body. The expanses of desert were hushed and black, filled with the shadows of the *saguaro* reaching up to the sky—she had no idea where she was, but she needed to get away. The panic within urged her to get up and flee, but her body still would not respond.

"I have given you a gift, one that many do not receive. The others who call on me or my kind, they're only puppets," he said, "but you could be my companion."

He stood only feet from her, looking down at the corpse of a man she knew would have killed her. She could now discern the shadows twisting about him, hideous shapes with elongated snouts and sharp nails.

"Don't fear me; accept it," he said.

Adriana's body was consumed with agony. She lay face-first in the dirt, fighting the pain. Within her mind, she could hear Dale's voice berating her.

"Dirty little bitch! I'm gonna fuck you after you're dead!"

He was still there, only inside of her now, his angry spirit screaming, choking her, slowly killing her just like he'd wanted to do when he was alive. She looked to the stranger, who grinned in the darkness; she could see the outline of sharp white teeth, the mouth of a predator who had his prey just where he wanted it.

"You can still hear him, feel him, like a maggot under your skin."

The stranger had deposited Dale's angry spirit there, leaving her no choice but to accept the offering, the curse he forced upon her.

"Take my hand, child. End your suffering," the stranger said.

She lifted her dirty face to see he was holding his hand out to her.

"Walk with me for a while."

Adriana placed her hand in his; it reminded her of clasping her brother Frankie's at his open-casket funeral, firm but devoid of life. The shadows leapt from his body. They ran down her arm, swarming over her.

Tenebrous hands found her mouth, fingernails like pinpricks pulling her jaws apart. They crawled down her throat like a cold fog, extinguishing the fiery pain, devouring Dale's insidious spirit.

"Now that they dwell inside of you, you must keep them fed," the stranger said. "The task won't be difficult, believe me."

"Feed them?" she questioned.

"They eat darkness," he answered.

"Darkness?" she asked.

"Don't worry, dear. There is plenty to satisfy them with there." His finger pointed to the lights of Apache Wells in the distance. "I'm sure that doesn't surprise you."

Adriana's eyes fell upon the city in the dessert, her hometown. It was the white trash armpit of southern Arizona. The stranger was correct: beyond the bright city lights there was plenty of darkness, plenty of food for whatever he'd left inside her with a kiss.

"Stand, Adriana. Let the night guide you."

All at once she moved over the desert floor like a cold, dark wind.

# THE GREAT HUNGER

RITCHIE CLAIMED THE truck stop restroom as his exclusive territory. It was a mighty fine place for getting high and crashing out; it even had air conditioning. On occasions he allowed folks to take shits in there when he was feeling generous. It kept Paul, the owner of the property, off his back, but the night he saw a little half-naked Mexican gal standing beyond the parking lot lights. he was in a nasty mood.

"Get your skanky ass outta here before the pigs are called," he hollered.

He had been waiting three hours for Ernie to hook him up, but the lazy fuck still hadn't come through. His insides were twisting like he'd swallowed a handful of hot maggots and his fuse was shorter than usual, which meant on a scale from one to ten he was at an eleven on the agitated asshole meter. He kicked at the gravel with the toe of his boot as if shooing away a stray dog, but the bitch didn't move. She just stood there beyond the flickering circle cast by the parking lot light high up on its pole.

"I said, get the fuck out of here. Don't you speak English, tortilla eater?" Ritchie didn't even bother pulling his shirt from his back pocket where it dangled. He stomped right across the gravel parking lot in only a pair of cut-off Levi's and his snake skin boots. Grasshoppers bounced off his chest as they performed midflight dances in the yellow light.

"What is it with you border jumpers?" He motioned erratically at her bare body. "You can't stand around with your tits hangin' out. This ain't Tia-fuckin-juana!"

He glanced nervously over his shoulder. No one had noticed her yet, but they would soon. A big old' Mormon wagon had just pulled up, packed to the ceiling with missionaries gearing up to cross the border. Ritchie stepped closer to her, yanked his shirt out of his pocket, and held it out to her

"Take the fuckin' thing and put it on!"

The girl didn't move, only stared at him with her dark eyes. She had bruises on her throat, and dirt was caked to her skin. If he had been one of those churchgoers he might have asked if she had been hurt, but all he could think about was making her go away before the red and blues came. Ernie sure as hell wouldn't be slinging shit if he caught sight of the police. Ritchie inched closer, waving the tattered shirt.

"Put this on," he said through gritted tooth shards, as he attempted to rein in his temper.

He held the shirt up over her head, stretching its collar wide as he would when dressing a child. The girl took a step backwards, nearly colliding with a creosote bush.

"Don't play fuckin' games with me!" Ritchie warned.

He followed her, then grabbed her by the jaw in order to show her to stay still. She looked into his eyes; the edges of hers swam with a blackness that steadily consumed them. He shook his head, looked at her again. His eyes weren't being deceived by the lack of smack in his veins; her eyes were totally black, not a bit of white in them. Her lips parted, and even in the darkness beyond the parking lot he could see something like black smoke twisting between her lips. Ritchie released her, then spun on his heels to get away from the demonic *senorita*, and ran right into the chest of a white man, also nearly naked.

"What the fuck is goin' on? Is that your bitch, bro? I wasn't doin' anything to her."

The stranger placed his hand over Ritchie's entire face to silence the drug addict, who was on the verge of losing his mind. The junkie struggled to free himself, only to feel the grip on his skull tighten until a painful crunch echoed in his own ears, radiating from his skull as it was compacted into his brain.

"Feed them, Adriana."

She was guided by an unnatural instinct; her body moved without heeding the tiny voice in the back of her mind that begged her to stop. Her hands gripped Ritchie's throat, and he twitched a bit as she put her mouth close to his. The taste of tooth decay and sour beer met her tongue, but what followed was like ambrosia, sinfully sweet, a forbidden delight she was never meant to experience. Upon tasting it she was struck with a ravenous hunger, a great hollow pain that needed to be fulfilled. In her mind she could hear Ritchie screaming, and in an instant his memories became hers, every seedy moment of his life, every secret he kept locked in the recesses of his mind. Her stomach squirmed as his spirit writhed within her. He fought against her ribcage, his prison, but his strength soon faded. She could feel that he was gone, and her stomach was empty once more. The drifter took Ritchie's lifeless body and tossed it into the creosote bushes like a limp mannequin.

"We are one now: you are me and I am you, black eyes."

His words rustled a memory in her mind, and for a moment she could nearly grasp it, but a rumbling in her stomach made her forget everything. She cared only to satisfy her cravings; she needed more of the darkness within people.

"Come now, before the sun catches us," he whispered.

She took his hand as he guided her back into the black expanse of the desert. Coyotes yipped and growled from the edges of a small hill, attempting to keep the new predators at bay but too frightened to come close to the two floating shadows.

"The beasts cannot harm you, they dare not defy me."

They spied a glow on the horizon, an orange orb of light: a campfire. Adriana felt her insides rolling, her gut rumbling, and the hole within her stomach expanding until it could hold many more like Ritchie.

"I'm so hungry."

"Your torment ends where that firelight shines."

\*\*\*

Consuelo fell to her knees before her bed, whispering every prayer she could remember, imploring every deity and spirit to protect her granddaughter. Every time she closed her eyes she could see the Shadow Man, his smiling face, a handsome monster she knew from when she was only a young woman. From her point of view she seemed to be gazing through Adriana's eyes. There was a bright light, almost blinding, and a campfire in the middle of utter darkness. Three men sat around it, unaware they were being hunted.

"No, Adriana..."

She was then flying through the air, her arms out before her, as a man retreated into the desert. He left the protection of his fire. His companions were screaming, their voices carrying through the night. Her hands were on him, her nails digging into his scalp at the back of his head. She yanked downward, and a horrid tearing sound like an old sheet ripping filled her ears. His blood washed over her, but she craved more than the red river rushing down his back. She spun him around, his face a mask of agony and horror. She moved with great speed and strength and broke his neck.

"She is strong. Your granddaughter has already tasted a soul," a familiar voice said, taunting her.

"No."

"She will reign over Pandemonium with me, as you promised you would long ago. Our kingdom will be historic, horrific." The Shadow Man's words echoed in her mind.

Consuelo forced herself to pull away in an attempt to break the psychic bonds she had with her granddaughter. *Hombre Sombra* was no longer a thing haunting her nightmares; he was flesh again. A single drop of blood ran from her nose and landed on her white bedsheet, spreading out in a red circle as it soaked into the soft linen.

"I have found you, black eyes." His voice was in her mind.

Consuelo fell forward, her bed catching her and cradling her head from bouncing off the tile floor. Tears of rage and fear blurred her eyes. The heavy mantle of shame she had managed to cast aside after many years was crawling over her once more. Her greatest failure had unearthed itself and was breathing again. She couldn't stand to witness anymore, the tainting of Adriana was too much to bear. Her hand strayed to the scars beneath her nightgown. The old wounds never fully healed, even after so many years. They were opening again, weeping in recollection of the torment she'd endured and of knowing what Adriana faced.

The demons housed in the prostitute at the truck stop were nothing compared to what was taking over Adriana. They couldn't pass into the human realm until after midnight, but the Shadow Man could break through as soon as the sun set, and once he had his claws into a victim, it wouldn't be long before he could walk in broad daylight. She didn't know what human host he had claimed as his own vessel, but she was certain he was now grooming her granddaughter to become his unholy companion, his bride in blasphemy.

The wooden box was on her nightstand; she had left it there to grant her strength and remind her of every dark thing she had already endured. She opened it and ran her fingers over the crucifix; it was marred by the blood of demons, most recently the one housed in the prostitute at the truck stop. Her heart stuttered as a tear traced down her cheek. The holy relic pulsed beneath her fingertips, and her link to Adriana was finally broken. The old woman stood and went to her phone book in the kitchen. Juan had left his cell number with her. She needed to get ahold of the gringo, Roy. There was a pinprick of light in his soul. She had witnessed it when he fought for his life against the possessed prostitute, and she would need it to save her grandchild.

*** 

Adriana was lying on a flat rock when dawn began to brighten the horizon. The shadowy stranger was already gone. He had left her with a kiss and a whispered promise of seeing her again. Her head ached and her throat was dry. She attempted to sit up, but her abdomen cramped, and she whimpered as she lay back down. She weakly fumbled with her shirt and skirt, both filthy and torn. She couldn't remember everything she did, but recalled bits and pieces of it. For a moment she refused to believe she had killed anyone, but she was far too familiar with what hid in the shadows. She cried softly, a feeling of self-loathing bubbling in her sore gut. She was a disgrace to her grandmother. She had fallen victim to the lure of the night and allowed herself to be controlled by it...by him.

"*No es tu culpa, mija.*"

The old woman's voice spoke softly in Adriana's mind, but she couldn't help but feel guilty. She couldn't force away the shame of being a monster—an unwilling one, but a monster all the same.

"*Voy por ti, aguanta.*"

Consuelo's voice was loud and clear in Adriana's mind, and while she didn't want to speak the truth to her grandmother, she knew she didn't have to. The old woman already knew.

"*Lo siento.*" Adriana wept.

The sun battered her skin, and flies came to gather around her. She shooed them away with a weak hand and waited. She could feel her grandmother was near; she would carry Adriana to safety, away from the waiting desert. Adriana's throat was parched, and her face burned with such exposure to the bright sun, but what hurt the most was her heart. Her conscience was eating her alive.

"*Estoy aqui.*"

A soft hand came to shield her watering eyes from the midday sun. Adriana looked up into her grandmother's face, and all at once had never felt so happy or ashamed in her whole life.

"*Ven, ayudame,*" Consuelo said, back over her shoulder, and Juan came to her side.

He knelt down and took Adriana's hand, his eyes filled with concern. "*Vamos a casa,*" Consuelo said.

\*\*\*

Adriana lay on the bed, sweating and trembling. Consuelo watched over her, fear eating her alive. She hadn't protected Adriana as she should have. Performing such a powerful exorcism ritual was something she hadn't done in years, because she knew her power would be like a beacon to her old foe. She knew the Shadow Man enlisted humans to be his eyes and ears in the earthly realm, and she had given herself away. She'd had a suspicious feeling ever since their encounter with El Gusano. She thought he was nothing more than a second-rate *brujo* who, like many, didn't compare to his reputation. The old woman had been dead wrong, and now he had a hand in corrupting the most treasured thing in her life.

Adriana cried out softly, and Consuelo held her hand in hopes of transferring a bit of her strength to the young woman. Consuelo knew the torment Adriana was going through, because she had lived through it once and had been lucky to survive. A soft whining drew her attention; she looked to the bedroom door. Their dog stood there, his hair rising on his back and a growl rumbling from his belly. His eyes were fixed on Adriana.

\*\*\*

Adriana was lost inside her own mind in visions of blood and darkness from times long before her birth. His presence filled her with ecstasy and terror all at once. He was dressed in a black suit, and stood beneath the arms of a withered tree on the roadside of somewhere far away from where she was born. She tried to speak, but found herself voiceless. He stepped into the light of the full moon, and its rays fell on the features of his face. He was handsome, but dangerous. It made her ache for him. As he grew closer to her, she could see his eyes were completely black. It struck fear in her heart like the tolling of a bell, but she couldn't turn away from his gaze. She was drawn to him by a pull stronger than the ocean tides. She was helpless and knew she would drown in him.

"Come closer, black eyes. Don't fear me. You and I are one and the same."

Adriana walked into his arms, and he wrapped them around her waist and drew her in to kiss him. His lips were cold, his breath was like a tomb, and yet she yearned for him. His teeth drew blood from her lips as his kiss grew rough and animalistic. Her breath became his as if they shared the same lungs, each clinging to the other for life. He drew back and smiled down at her, his teeth sharp, his grin like a wolf's under the moon.

"You are mine," he whispered with the voice of a beast.

# DEBTS TO PAY

HE SAT ON the floor of his trailer drinking a tallboy of Old Milwaukee. He had completed his task for the week: the rooster cages had been taken elsewhere, as he was no longer their keeper. Chamuco had sent a new guy to his place to make sure he was up to his new task. Roy was going to become a drug mule, whether he really wanted to or not. Chamuco knew his promise to find information on Cuervo would be impossible for the gringo so he assigned him a new job. Hector had been correct when he said his boss would have more lucrative employment opportunities for Roy besides just being in charge of roosters, but Roy was too stupid to realize it would mean running cocaine across the border. He didn't want to sit on his couch or turn his lights on, fearing Cuervo's men might find out about his new line of work and drive by to blast a few holes through the thin walls of his double-wide. It was clear El Cuervo would consider him a traitor, and he knew sooner or later he'd pay for it. Some might call him a pussy for not facing his problems like a man, but they had obviously never been crammed into a meat freezer and forced to wait for someone to butcher them like a pig. Roy preferred to sit in the dark on his shag carpeting with a cheap beer than have his head suddenly burst like an overripe watermelon at the introduction of a bullet. He wore boxers and a black t-shirt—he hadn't gotten fully dressed since waking up with a headache and being instructed on running cocaine from Mexico to Arizona. He scratched at his thigh and focused on his leg; his wound was healing, but the memories remained. He reached over to a small table beside his couch where he had tossed Hector's bags of devil shit, one red and one black. He had no idea what they really contained, but they gave him an eerie feeling. Twice he had gone to throw them away but hesitated, and he didn't know why. He left them lying beside the lamp, its yellowed illumination casting a golden glow over them.

His door rattled with a knocking. Someone was on his front porch. Roy nearly shit himself before he heard Juan's voice.

"Roy? You home?"

"What the fuck do you want?" Roy asked, as he got up and glanced nervously out the window next to his door, nearly spilling his beer.

"*La curandera* needs you."

"Who?"

"The old woman."

Roy felt his stomach drop. He was grateful to her, but she was a memory he hoped to drink away.

"She needs *me?*" Roy asked suspiciously, and opened his door.

"The girl needs you, her granddaughter."

"Adriana?" he asked.

"*Sí.*"

Roy ran his hand through his unwashed hair anxiously and chugged his warm beer. His mind tumbled over the possibilities of why the old woman and her granddaughter would need him, and every one of them made him nervous.

"She needs *me?*"

"I said yes, *pendejo!*"

"Okay, let me put on my pants," Roy conceded. After they got the demon poison out of his leg wound, he couldn't refuse Consuelo or Adriana.

"Roy, bring the Ouija board."

"How did you know about it?"

"The old woman told me, she said she needs to cleanse it."

Roy grabbed the board and hesitated at the bags of devil shit on the table. He grabbed them, shoved them in his pocket, and headed out the door.

# ADRIANA

THE YOUNG WOMAN was still drenched in sweat, but her lips were pale and dry. Roy stood in the doorway to her bedroom and watched her grandmother hover over her, patting her forehead with a damp cloth that was soaking in a bowl full of sprigs of plants he couldn't identify. Roy held the Ouija board out, and Consuelo took it and left the room. Roy could hear the old woman speaking in a commanding voice, and as he looked back over his shoulder he could see her dousing the board with the contents of the same bowl. Smoke rose from the board, and she nodded in satisfaction.

"That doorway is closed forever. The true battle begins now," she said as she came back to stand beside Adriana.

The old woman took a large wooden crucifix and laid it on Adriana's chest. She bound it in place with a long strip of cloth that she wound about Adriana, just as she might wrap an injured arm in a sling. The lights were off but for a small lamp, and a handful of candles were lit on a mantel above the bed, each one representing saints Roy couldn't name, but their faces appeared brave and angelic, and they reminded him of Adriana. He stepped closer to her. Her dark eyes were closed and her breathing was shallow. Every once in a while she'd grimace, contorting her face with what he assumed was pain. He had spoken to Juan, who'd relayed to him Consuelo's concern that Adriana was possessed by a spirit far more deadly than the one that took over Wanda's body, and from what he saw, he thought she was right.

"What are we gonna do?" he whispered to Juan, who had pulled a flask from his pocket.

"Destroy it," he answered before taking a long drink.

"How the hell are we gonna fight something if we can't see it?" Roy asked.

"The grandmother knows the demon, she has battled it before. She has a plan."

Roy nodded and turned his back towards Consuelo, then asked softly, "Is she sure we can beat this thing?"

"She hopes we can," Juan said, as he continued to drink his liquid courage until it was gone.

"Hopes we can?"

"Don't be a coward, Roy. You, more than me, owe her your life."

"I am not a coward," Roy huffed.

"Then show me you have the balls, repay her what you owe her."

"I will. I always make good on my debts," Roy said.

# EL CUERVO

THE BLACK TRUCK parked down the street, but all eyes within it were focused on the small house. Cuervo knew Roy was inside; the *capo* had men following him. He grew tired of waiting to see if any of Chamuco's men came to his trailer. Roy had already been branded a traitor for being with Hector the day the *carniceria* was attacked, and Cuervo meant to kill him for it, but first he would torture the white boy until he gave up information about Chamuco and his whereabouts. The years of hiding his rancor had ended, and it was strangely liberating for Cuervo. Chamuco had broken the pact to operate in their own territories and on friendly terms, so now it was time to claim the entire pie instead of splitting it down the middle. Chamuco had conspired to kill Cuervo, and he wouldn't be forgiven. Cuervo was ready to end the war and send his rival to Hell where he belonged.

"*Listo, cabrones?*" Cuervo asked his men.

They drew their guns as the driver turned the truck around and parked in front of Consuelo's house.

# A PAINFUL TRADE

CHAMUCO BARELY HAD the strength to walk from his bedroom to the kitchen. The sunlight through the windows hurt his eyes. He felt as if he was hungover, but with a *crudo* so bad it could become deadly. His maid was standing at the stove, stirring a pot, not paying any attention to her patron when he came up behind her.

"*Que es?*"

She screamed and turned, cursing him, but only in her mind. She steadied herself, not wishing to anger Chamuco, especially since he looked sick. She kept reminding herself how David had gone missing, and how she, too, could disappear, and no one would ever know what happened to her.

"*Pozole, patron,*" she answered.

"*Que rico,*" he said unenthusiastically.

She squinted and took a long look at his face, then brought her hand to his cheek. He didn't have a fever, but she was still concerned, because he felt cold as ice.

"*Te sientes bien?*"

"*Si, si, solomente crudo.*"

"*Seguro?*"

"*Si,*" he said, irritation slipping into his voice. He was tired of her treating him like a child.

"*Tienes hambre?*"

"*No tengo hambre. Tengo sed.*"

She nodded, noticing his tone was growing stern, and turned back to cooking before she actually made him angry.

"*Y el Gusano, donde esta?*"

"*En el granero, patron,*" she answered, and watched him wander away like a lost spirit.

She had watched him grow older, the beast of greed festering inside of him since he was barely old enough to have chest hair. Marta had basically raised him and David as if they were her own sons. Her sister told her his uncle was dying of cancer, and the arrangement guaranteeing his young nephew territory in Arizona was in danger of being cast aside. She had heard him speaking to the *brujo* about Cuervo's meetings at the church; he had been worried he would be left with nothing. The women of the house were supposed to be blind and deaf to all conversations spoken about business, and for many years she was, but she miraculously regained her eyesight and hearing when David vanished. Marta could stand it no more.

\*\*\*

Chamuco walked to the back door and gazed out at the old barn. It had been on the property long before he'd ever bought it. He'd initially planned to tear it down, but after his chance meeting with the *Tres Gusanos* he left it standing, and before he knew it, it became their residence. He had offered them all rooms within his mansion, but they refused, favoring the idea of dwelling in the dark barn with its rotten timbers and splintered walls, like vermin in a den. Surrounding the dilapidated wooden structure were acres of desert soil, dry and barren. Nothing would grow there, and the only things planted there were the corpses of men he wished to silence. It was a field of death. That was where he took the form of the Shadow Man, a process he couldn't fully remember, just that his bones and hair grew longer, his body got thicker with muscle, and his mind became no longer his own.

Chamuco wished to speak to the *brujo,* but he halted there, hypnotized by the view of the landscape by daylight. The sun spilled in through the window, and it was irritating to his skin and eyes, but nothing compared to the torment his insides were going through. He hoped the pain would pass; he had lived through his first transformation, so maybe it would get easier. But something told him it wouldn't. He had housed the Shadow Man, let him run the night freely, but now his body was his own once more and Chamuco had business to conduct. He couldn't afford to feel like the walking dead every day of his existence, not if he meant to destroy El Cuervo.

Chamuco pulled his cellphone out of the pocket of his black bathrobe and prepared to call the soup man, but then the barn door swung open as if Gusano knew he would be summoned to the main house. Chamuco watched his personal *brujo* make his way towards him. El Gusano didn't wear a shirt, only black jeans, boots, and skin covered in tattoos of sacred texts and blasphemous symbols. His face was serious—a stark contrast to when he actually smiled or laughed—and his face looked like a hairless coyote, a hungry creature only mocking joyful responses to convince humans he wasn't plotting to cut them into pieces. Chamuco shuddered, and for a second he wondered what kind of monster he had welcomed into his home. The thought was dashed away when he remembered his willingness to breed such evil to wield for his own selfish purposes; it was a fair trade in his eyes. All men had a price, a currency to bargain their soul for, and his was power.

*** 

The twins watched from the shadow of the barn door, speaking telepathically and giggling at Chamuco's pain. It was palpable, and they absorbed it like sand soaking up blood. He had struck the deal with them, and the price he would pay would be horrifically exquisite. They knew he was now questioning El Gusano, asking him how long the suffering would last until Chamuco held his prized position, and the sly old *brujo* was assuring him it was only a matter of hours. They waited for nightfall, biding their time, knowing it wouldn't be long now—their work was nearly done.

# THE OLD KING

CUERVO AND HIS men busted down the door. They didn't bother keeping quiet because most of the neighbors were already in debt to them in one way or another. Roy greeted them with a raised pistol, but when he realized how many guns were pointed at him, he let his drop to the living room carpet.

"Don't move," Cuervo ordered as he pushed his way into Consuelo's house.

"I didn't plan on it," Roy said.

Cuervo motioned for his men to check the place out, and soon discovered Juan and Consuelo guarding Adriana. The party was moved to the bedroom, where Roy, Juan, and Consuelo were tied up while Cuervo showed mercy to the young woman in the bed, who was obviously very ill. He left her shaking and sweating under the blankets.

"Tell me, gringo, what plans does Chamuco have for me?" The old *capo* grinned knowingly.

"Hector said he wants to kill you and take your territory," Roy admitted. He didn't have any reason to lie, especially since Hector was dead and Chamuco hadn't come to offer him any money to keep quiet. Besides, he could see Cuervo eyeing the two women, obviously choosing which one he'd torture in front of Roy to get him to talk.

"And what did he promise you for changing sides?"

"I was never on anyone's side. I've worked with both of you for years. I raise roosters, that's all, nothing more, and I do it for other people too, some of them in cartels, some not. I'm really not a part of this world."

"That wasn't my question," Cuervo said, and grabbed Consuelo by the arm. He put his gun to her head and continued. "What did he offer you to make you go to my warehouse and shed blood?"

"I lost his rooster. Hector helped me find out who killed it, and when we found her, we had to make her pay."

"Yes, and that was Hector's plan. He wanted to go to my warehouse and start a war, but you still haven't answered my question. Are you deaf, or do you really want to see me shoot this bitch in the head?"

"Okay, okay. Hector offered me a job. He said they could use a gringo to help them get shit across the border from the other side."

"It doesn't take white skin and good English to do that. Look at me, I do that already, but it's because I have power. Sure, I'm bilingual and rich, but most importantly...people know what happens when they fuck with me."

"That's just what Hector said Chamuco could offer me, a better job," Roy said.

"And you accepted?"

"No, no, not really. I just wanted to clear up the problem with this rooster. I didn't want anything else."

"Liar!."

"NO!"

"How about I put a bullet in her instead?" He lowered his gun to just above Adriana's head.

"No, please. I swear I'm not involved in your world. I just wanted to avoid getting shot by Chamuco. I wasn't looking to join any war against you."

"Too late," Cuervo said, then brought his gun up and shot Juan in the shoulder.

"FUCK!" Roy cried. Juan had saved his life twice, once by opening the freezer and a second time by bringing him to the house of *la curandera*.

"This war has been coming for years, white boy. I felt it in my bones from the day we made the pact. I knew he would want it all. Tell me where he is!"

"I don't fucking know!"

"Don't be so loyal, tell me."

"This isn't about loyalty, I just really don't know."

"Not even a week ago my suspicions were confirmed when a priest told me a secret spoken to him in through confession: Chamuco was going to kill me. And guess what?"

"What?"

"He was murdered. That priest baptized Chamuco when he was just a baby, and that's how he was repaid by the sick bastard. My men found the priest's headless body on the side of the road... Do you think Chamuco won't do the same to you? He has no soul, no honor!"

"Then shoot him, not us!" Roy said.

"How can I find him, and more importantly, how do I kill him? I heard of the thing you brought with you to the freezer. It was a demon. He sent a demon to kill my men."

"I have no idea what that was, but the only way I survived was the old woman you're pointing a gun at."

"So it's true. Chamuco is using *brujeria* to kill me?"

"I have no idea, man. I just know he's supposed to be a fuckin' weird dude. Hector warned me about him. I don't know if he worships the devil or fuckin' Santa Claus."

Cuervo ran his hand over his face in exhaustion. "We're getting nowhere here."

"I don't know what you want me to say."

"I feel like I'm in one of those stories of old kings and how they were constantly challenged by young men for their power. But what these fools need to remember is that old men like me are the most dangerous, because we have done terrible things in order to live so long in this business."

Roy was growing tired of the speeches and waxing philosophical with a guy who was glorifying selling cocaine, making it seem majestic like he was a wizard of smack or the King Arthur of nose candy. Roy just wanted to stick a gun in Cuervo's asshole and empty the clip into his colon. Juan coughed and gripped his wound; his pain was growing with each heartbeat. Each passing minute he wasn't in a hospital would only lessen his chances of living, and Roy knew it.

Adriana moaned, a deep rattling breath, and fidgeted beneath her blankets. Cuervo looked at her, then around the room. His eyes went wide. "What's wrong with her? Is she a demon too?"

"No, she's just sick!" Roy said, worried Cuervo would get paranoid and put a bullet in Adriana's head. "Leave her alone!"

"*Hijos de putas*," Juan groaned, and gripped his shoulder.

"Juan." Consuelo wept and reached out to the injured man.

"*Disculpame, doña*," Cuervo said, then motioned to his men, who grabbed Roy and the other three.

"I still need to be certain she isn't a demon, and unfortunately for you, there is only one way of doing that. And if what you said was true, I'll need the old woman," he said as he exited the room.

# A SHADOW WITH TEETH

ROY FOUND HIMSELF back in the freezer of the *carniceria* with his hands bound behind his back. Consuelo and Adriana were taken somewhere else, but he and Juan were sent to freeze their balls off until Cuervo decided his next move. He worried about Consuelo after he admitted she was the one who put Wanda down. He didn't know what Cuervo would do with her.

"Does he think Chamuco is gonna come to our rescue? He's gonna break in like a *narco* Batman and try to set us free or some shit?"

Juan didn't answer. He just gripped his bloody shoulder and tried not to move.

"I haven't even met the guy. He doesn't give a rat fuck about me."

"*Callate*, Roy."

Juan was in pain; it was obvious in his face. He kept his eyes and jaw clenched in concentration, trying to put his mind somewhere else, a place where he wasn't in agony.

"Are you okay?" Roy asked.

"No, gringo. This isn't a fucking movie where a guy gets shot and he continues to fire machine guns and climb trees. I have a hole in my shoulder and it fucking hurts."

"Sorry, buddy. We're gonna get out of this."

"Just shut up, please," Juan pleaded.

Roy fell silent and glanced around him. He didn't see Hector's corpse, but remembering the first time he was put in the freezer was like recalling a living nightmare. His eyes scanned the frosty surroundings, fearful of catching any movement among the pieces of frozen dead things. His battle with Wanda was something he never wanted to experience again, so he refused to be taken by surprise or find Juan eaten by a spindly whore-beast like Hector was. He would keep watch until Cuervo opened the door again, and when he did Roy planned on fighting his way to freedom. He would drag Juan along with him, and repay the debt he owed him for saving his ass from Wanda.

\*\*\*

Adriana was laid out on the floor of the warehouse. They had wrapped her in a blanket, but that was the only comfort they afforded her. Consuelo was tied to a chair and ignored while a group of men drank beer and played cards. Cuervo had disappeared somewhere in the gigantic building, leaving his hostages to the care of his men. Hours passed by like days and Consuelo counted each minute in her mind. When her internal count had nearly marked nightfall, Adriana's body jerked upright and she sat with her eyes wide open, staring beyond the shocked men who went for their pistols. Consuelo took a deep breath and choked back the fear she had for her beloved grandchild. The battle laid out before her would be treacherous, and Adriana would be lucky to survive.

"Que te pasa, pinche loca?" a gunman asked.

"La noche la llama," Consuelo whispered.

The man nearest the exit looked out the great steel door, baffled by how the old woman knew the sun was setting outside. There were no windows in the warehouse, no clocks on the walls.

A gurgling screech issued from Adriana's gaping mouth, and she tore at the bindings on her chest. The crucifix was thrown to the concrete floor and skidded beneath a steel table, out of sight and forgotten by all but Consuelo as the gunmen armed themselves and stepped back from the young woman staring at them. They were aware of the fight between Wanda's possessed body and their fellow members of Cuervo's cartel; stories of that horrific battle spread like wildfire amongst the chismosos of the gang. These men wanted nothing to do with Adriana or whatever demon she had inside her. The bravest of the bunch ran for his cellphone, which was sitting on a case of beer, but before he could call for help, Adriana was flying toward him. She moved with inhuman speed, her feet didn't even appear to touch the ground. She swung her fist, and it connected with his throat and punctured a hole in his windpipe. A fountain of blood bathed her, invigorated her lust to kill. The man gripped his throat and fought to breathe, but it was all in vain. Two others opened fire, spraying the warehouse full of bullets, but not one hit Adriana as she nimbly evaded them. She was a shadow with teeth, springing on them and opening their veins with her fingernails.

Consuelo pushed her chair backward across the floor with her feet to escape the ricocheting lead, but she only managed to fall backwards onto the concrete, leaving herself prone to both gunfire and an attack by her own granddaughter. She couldn't see Adriana as she attacked the last three men, but she could hear the sickening snapping of bones and the wet ripping of flesh, and she knew the young woman could not hold back the darkness inside of her.

Cuervo ran into the warehouse, his gun ready. He expected to be met by Chamuco's men, or maybe find Roy had escaped the freezer, but what he saw made his heart stutter in his chest. The girl was eating his men alive.

"*Puta madre!*"

He fired at Adriana, hitting her in the back. She spun to face him, betraying no trace of pain from the hole he'd left in her. Her dark eyes were completely black now, and her mouth dripped blood down onto her chest. He fired again, but this time she was expecting it, and she dodged his bullets until his pistol was empty. He turned to run, but she caught him by the back of his hair and yanked him back. While they struggled, Consuelo managed to free her hands from the ties behind her back. She crawled over to retrieve the sacred crucifix, and a shower of Cuervo's blood rained down on her, bathing her in the warmth of his escaping life. Adriana bit into his throat, burying her teeth in his Adam's apple; then, with a vicious jerk of her head, she tore free a mouthful of flesh. Consuelo held her breath and prayed in her mind as she crept away to rescue Roy and Juan; after witnessing Adriana's strength, she knew she couldn't face her granddaughter alone.

\*\*\*

The freezer door opened, and Roy expected to see his executioner coming with a gaudy gold gun to put a bullet through his head, spreading his hot blood and brain matter out across the walls of his frozen prison. Instead, it was a little old woman with serious dark eyes. He was flooded with relief as Consuelo came to him and began untying his hands. Juan's labored breathing came out in thin clouds in the cold air, but he was conscious and not ready to die in the freezer of the *carniceria*.

"*Ayudame, por favor.*"

"*Un minuto,*" Consuelo said, as she helped Roy to his feet.

He pulled Juan up and Consuelo worked on his bindings.

"We're getting out of here," Roy promised.

They wrapped their arms around Juan's waist and made their way to the freezer door.

"Wait, don't go too fast, they'll kill us," Roy whispered.

"No they won't," Consuelo said.

Roy looked to her with confusion so she told him the truth. "Adriana has killed them all."

Screams met them as they stepped into the warehouse attached to the back of the *carniceria* and *mercado*, but they didn't come from anywhere near them. The cries of terror were coming from within the market itself, where the bright colors, discount vegetables, and fluorescent lights beckoned to all the people of the neighborhoods surrounding it. Adriana wasn't satisfied with slaughtering the men of the cartel, she had moved on to innocent people. Consuelo's head swam with the terrors of her past, of awakening to the taste of human blood in her mouth.

"No, Adriana, no!"

"What is going on?" Roy asked.

"The demon, he is opening a door to hell, and Adriana is helping him."

# DAVID

CHAMUCO WATCHED THE horizon turn red with the setting of the sun. His time in control of himself was about to be relinquished once more. El Gusano came to collect him and lead him back out into the field of death. The *brujo* had a smile on his face, but his eyes were still dead.

The twin *brujas* awaited them, their filthy cloth dresses fluttering in the wind like burial shrouds.

Chamuco felt a painful, hollow spot in his gut. It intensified with each step he took toward the field of death until he could hardly stand on his own. Gusano grabbed Chamuco by his upper arms before he fell to his knees, and helped him move forward to where the *bruja* with warts ringing her mouth was already tugging a corpse free of the earth.

Chamuco recognized the decayed body. It was his former head of security, David. Chamuco had ordered him dead after he defied an order to kill a priest. A chill ran through Chamuco, and his body refused to move. Gusano pushed him forward, his bony fingers tight around Chamuco's arms. The *brujo* stood a head taller than him, and even though Chamuco's body had more muscle, Gusano moved him easily.

David's body was laid out on the sand. He was dressed in only his bloodstained underwear. His clothing had been stripped off during the hours of torture in which he'd confessed to telling the priest of Chamuco's plot to kill Cuervo. David's refusal to relinquish his antiquated code of honor did him in. The fairy tale in his mind about how *narcos* should conduct business—spending hours negotiating to squash beef instead of making the sky rain bullets over every single argument—was one instilled in him by his father, who'd also died defending the ideology of the old guard. In his eyes, Chamuco should have upheld the pact he made with his competition and continued to live in peace with Cuervo while working in separate territories. David had been a dreamer ever since he was a kid, when Chamuco had befriended him, but Chamuco was not a dreamer, he was a taker. He always craved more than what he had.

The twin *brujas*, like fattened maggots, knelt and ran their hands over David's rotting flesh. His skin split as they dug their jagged nails into him. They whispered words in a language Chamuco couldn't place. Even with his stint studying *satanismo* in an attempt to gain supreme power, their incantations were far beyond his limited knowledge. Their garbled voices grew in volume and intensity as they stripped the flesh from David's torso, and their eyes took on a yellow light, like the moon was shining through their skulls.

El Gusano forced Chamuco to his knees. The agonizing pain in his stomach was almost unbearable. He felt like he was being eaten alive from the inside out. He tried not to let his agony show through on his face, he wanted to portray the look of a stone-cold motherfucker, but in his mind he questioned whether or not he'd survive the emergence of the Shadow Man again. He consciously asked if this was all his life would hold for him, now and forever—kneeling naked in the sand beside a corpse, waiting to be bathed in its fluids, and feeling the agony of *El Hombre Sombra* taking control.

He watched the brujas plunge their filthy hands into David's abdomen, separating his innards from the rotting cavity hiding them. A sea of maggots overflowed onto the sand as they pulled them free. His mind flashed to memories of him and David when they were just teenagers. His friend's body was strong and youthful then, not the nightmare of fetid anatomy it was now. David had been trustworthy with Chamuco's secrets, and had fought alongside him at parties when they got too drunk and mouthy with the older guys. Chamuco felt his throat tighten, but he refused to shed a tear, not for a traitor.

"*Es tiempo*," Gusano said.

Once more he was baptized in putrid juices from his head to his feet. All he had left of David beyond his childhood memories ran down his cheeks and stung his eyes. Chamuco kept his mouth tightly shut, not wanting to taste death on his tongue, but its essence crept up his nostrils and sank into his skin until Chamuco felt as if he was a corpse himself.

*Los Tres Gusanos* laughed when he lost consciousness and fell face-first into David's corpse. One of the twin *brujas* rolled him off it into the dirt, and the three stood over him, waiting for their true master to emerge.

Chamuco's skin went cold and grey, the pallor of death. His body took on the appearance of the Shadow Man's favorite disguise. He was never human, but an entity of ancient times, a demon of Lucifer's army.

He could choose a different form each time he was brought to flesh, but this would be recognizable to the woman he sought, and to her grandmother. He opened his black eyes and laughed as he gazed upon himself. Adriana would welcome him with open arms, and Consuelo would cower in remembrance of him.

He could feel Adriana on the horizon, her heart beating rapidly as she hunted, as she slaughtered. The Shadow Man needed to join her before she realized she was not immortal like him, nearly unstoppable but still able to perish. Her human body could die, and with it would go her damned soul. His spirit was eternal, a cycle of malevolence that could be reborn a million times in his quest to open the gates of Hell on Earth. He walked naked to the back door of Chamuco's mansion and let himself inside; he needed to dress himself so he wouldn't draw the attention of the people of Apache Wells before he transformed the city into a place of demons and everlasting suffering, Pandemonium. Its meaning, *all demons*, an abode for Satan himself. The Shadow Man had placed the name into the sleeping brain of a poet, who wrote it into existence to plague the minds of humankind with nightmares of a city of death and damnation. Its meaning had changed over the centuries, morphed into a lesser threat of a wild uproar or lawless situation, but he adored its true meaning more and he intended for every man and woman of Apache Wells to know it intimately.

# MARTA

SHE SAT ON David's bed, holding a picture he used to have on the bedside table. It was of him and his father. Marta remembered David's father fondly. When she was younger, she'd even found herself in his bed a few times, as she had with quite a few men of his trade. Both David and his father held a quality she could only describe as gentlemanly. Marta wasn't stupid, she knew what they did for a living, but they both still had morals, even amongst the darkness they dealt in. They had codes, they followed them, and their word as men was always kept. She felt a swell of sadness in her chest as her eyes grew teary. Those days were long gone, and all she was left with now was a house filled with evil.

She looked out the window and could see Chamuco's men, just like another night she would never forget, when she watched Chamuco walking naked beneath the moon. His men stood there on the perimeter of the property, holding their guns like statues. Motionless, they stood around in a daze as if they had been hypnotized. She knew it was the work of the *brujo* and the twins. She had no definite idea as to why Chamuco would turn his small army into mindless zombies, but she was certain it had to do with his new companions and whatever secret plans they whispered about in the barn.

Marta didn't know what to do, but she was certain of one thing: she was sick of it all, and would no longer sit by and watch it happen. She tucked the picture into her apron and went to David's closet. She stood on her tiptoes and felt along a high shelf until her fingertips found something cold and heavy—the barrel of a gun.

***

She could hear his footsteps, and he spoke to himself with the voice of a stranger. She gripped the rifle and hesitated for a moment, whispering a quick prayer before pushing her way into his bedroom. Marta lifted the gun and pointed it at the closet as he stepped out. She froze in confusion at the appearance of a man she had never seen before. His eyes were on her, and they were black as night.

"Marta," the stranger spoke.

She felt a chill run through her body, and her heart stammered.

"You don't know me, but I know you," he said, creeping forward. "Yo te conosco, Marta," he whispered, and she felt a frigid cold settle in her bones.

She gripped the gun with all of her strength, but her arms trembled uncontrollably. He smiled. His mouth was like a wolf's, teeth long and pointed. She felt her heart seizing in her chest as he came for her.

*** 

Gusano heard the gunshot but sauntered slowly towards the house. Their men were already under Chamuco's control; the *brujo* had made certain of it before they ever began his transformation rituals. The only one who ever resisted was David, but he was silenced by the bony hands of *la calaca*. The gunshot could only have come from one person: the housemaid, Marta. It really wasn't a surprise to him; she had always looked on him like he was a *lacra*. And she was right: he was nothing but a leech, a plague looking for more corpses to devour. He truly only answered to one master—*El Hombre Sombra*, the Shadow Man. They used Chamuco only as a way to bring him back to the flesh.

Gusano walked through the kitchen and grinned at the sound of muffled wailing coming from upstairs. The old woman would no longer be around to clean and cook, but once Pandemonium was brought to the world, the master would only sup from languishing souls and the sweet taste of endless suffering, making her services no longer required. With each step up the stairs he could hear her struggling, and as he approached the open bedroom door, Gusano could see her splayed out on the bed with the Shadow Man sitting on her. Her throat was open, and blood ran from the Shadow Man's pointed teeth as he looked down into her dying eyes.

"*Saluda me al David en el infierno.*"

# OJOS NEGROS

SHERIFF LANCASTER LEANED against the wall, the pressure in his hip abated a bit. He had been sitting in his patrol car too long again. He hadn't slept much since the killing spree. One junkie dead at a truck stop and a camp of vagrants left slain in the desert just a few miles away made for a very busy night for him. He didn't have a chance to get any healing from the girls at the truck stop. It didn't concern him as much as it pissed him off. There had been too many deaths recently, and it was making him look bad. His agreement with the local cartels stated they would shed no blood within the city limits, at least not in the form of shredded corpses. He would need to remind them of his worth as an ally.

"This won't look good come re-election time."

"Shove it up your ass, Lisa," the sheriff said to the coroner.

"This isn't all. You know the priest was killed too. We never found his head. And then the growing list of missing persons..."

"Don't concern yourself with those people until they're stretched out on one of your cold steel tables."

She nodded. "Whatever you say."

"Let's get down to it, tell me how they died."

"They were all attacked by someone. Their bodies are ravaged: broken bones, bashed skulls, and severe internal trauma."

"Is this an animal? You said something attacked them."

"I said someone. There are fingerprints on the bodies," she answered.

"Did we run them against the database?"

"One of your detectives is on that, but if the suspect hasn't been arrested before, you're out of luck."

"Tell me something I don't know."

"Okay, their insides are already in advanced stages of decay, as if their guts had been dead for days before the rest of them died."

"What the fuck would do that? A disease of some sort? A new type of drug they consumed?"

"I would consider those explanations, but it wouldn't explain the physical attacks they endured. They were obviously murdered."

"Don't make me do your fuckin' job, Lisa. Maybe these crackheads downed some sort of new narcotic, got all whacked out, and killed each other. Take another look inside of them."

Lisa tilted her head, thought for a moment, and smiled. "Seems a little outlandish, but I've seen some weird shit in my time. I'll open them up again."

"All right, keep me informed. I gotta get outta here, it gives me the creeps."

She watched him hobble his way out of her office before taking a seat at her desk. She needed a break before getting back to work. Her coffee mug had gone cold, but she sipped it anyway. Her mind turned over the multitude of explanations for her freezer being crammed full of suspicious deaths. She decided she'd call Ernestina in Phoenix the following morning; she had more experience than Lisa, and in the big city she had seen an assortment of odd deaths. Lisa was also interested in knowing if Phoenix was turning up with dead men who seemed to be rotten before they drew their last breaths, too.

Minnie passed by her office door, and Lisa got to her feet. Her younger assistant was just clocking in, and had no idea of the work they had ahead of them.

"I hope you're ready to pull our new guests out of the cooler and take another look," she said, trailing behind Minnie.

"I figured we weren't finished with them." Minnie sighed. "Maybe this time we'll find a clue as to how they were done in."

"I'm calling Phoenix tomorrow, Ernestina may have an idea."

"Wouldn't be the first time she gave us a hand, that woman has seen some shit," Minnie said, as she suited up to begin a night of being elbow-deep in the dead.

\*\*\*

They hauled Ritchie, the junkie, out onto the table first.

"Let's look through what's left of this gentleman here. I'm sure he was only minding his business when he got his skull crushed behind a seedy truck stop bathroom," Lisa said sarcastically.

"I'm sure he was a prize when he was alive." Minnie pointed out a tattoo of a crooked swastika. "Looks like it was done in the joint, or someone's garage."

"His insides were black with decay when we first cut him open, let's see if there are any signs of it being from something he consumed."

Minnie and Lisa stood on either side of Ritchie's corpse and began opening his abdomen again. His internal organs had already been removed, and since they seemed out of the ordinary, they were also stored in the walk-in refrigerator. The gaping hole emitted a strong odor of rot, and the tissue inside the cavity was green and slimy. Minnie backed away.

"This is NOT normal!"

Lisa was shocked. Her eyes were so focused on the abnormal state of decomposition, she didn't notice Ritchie's eyes opening amidst the carnage of his crushed skull. His once-blue eyes were completely black.

Minnie screamed, startling Lisa from her concentration.

"He's moving!" Minnie yelped, and pointed to Ritchie, but his hand shot out to grab Lisa's arm before she could move.

Lisa tried to yank her arm back, but he wouldn't release her. Ritchie sat forward, his mouth falling open and unearthly screams filling the coroner's ears. She punched him in his disfigured face and broke free from his grip. He pulled himself off the exam table and continued to scream, his arms stretched out, reaching for the two women. The table and Ritchie were between them and the exit. They backed away until their backs were against the freezer door.

"We gotta hide in here, come on," Lisa said, and turned to unlock the heavy steel door, but once she turned the latch she heard something on the other side.

More screeching cries.

# PATH OF CARNAGE

ROY AND CONSUELO stopped at the employee entrance at the back of the Rancho Grande Carniceria and Mercado. It was a giant building, housing a variety of grocery and household items, with the capacity to hold hundreds of people at a time. It was open twenty-four hours a day and it was usually extremely busy, and this night was no different. They looked out across the store to see total chaos, *es un desmadre de sangre y muerte*. Women lay bleeding and weeping. Children hid beneath displays for California avocados and fabric softener, their eyes wide after discovering that monsters were real. A stock boy with his arm torn from its socket stumbled toward them, begging for help, and it had all happened in a matter of minutes.

Juan steadied himself against the wall. His shoulder was still in agony, and he didn't know how long he could hold on without going to a hospital. When Consuelo opened the door to the shopping area of the Rancho Grande and Juan caught a glimpse of the carnage inflicted by Adriana, he nearly fell to the floor. Roy turned to Consuelo, his eyes asking her what the hell they were supposed to do.

"*Sigueme.*"

Loud screams from somewhere in the store shook the *curandera*. Juan could see her hands trembling, but she stepped beyond the threshold of the double-doors and held a crucifix out before her. Her bravery ignited his own, fanning it from a dwindling ember into a bright flame once more. He stood straighter and pushed his pain into the back of his mind. Roy followed Consuelo, with Juan behind him, and the three were ready to do battle with the evil that held Adriana in its thrall. They had just exited the hallway leading to the warehouse when Cuervo's dead gunmen came stumbling behind them, their mouths hanging wide open, their eyes black orbs, and their voices transformed to a chorus of demonic wailing.

The three ran into the store. Consuelo turned around, holding the crucifix out before her. The dead men fell back a few steps, hissing and swiping at the wooden cross, but they were still too close. She glanced around, frantically seeking a weapon against the possessed men. Her eyes found what she needed to beat the demons back long enough to destroy them.

"*La sal!*" the old woman cried to her companions cowering behind her.

"The salt! Grab it!" Juan said to Roy.

Roy took a step toward the end of an aisle where a display was erected, but the demonic gunmen lurched at him. Consuelo stepped between them and beat the nearest one across the face with the crucifix. His face seared instantly, and stinking smoke permeated the air. Roy grabbed a bag of salt, tore it open, and swung it. A wave of it fell across their attackers, and they fell back screaming in agony; like acid rain, it burned holes through their flesh. Consuelo took advantage of their weakened state and used the crucifix like a dagger, plunging it into their hearts. Their crying stopped and they moved no more. The black in their eyes receded, and their stares were only those of dead men once more.

"Is everyone she killed going to end up like that?" Roy asked.

"*Si*," Consuelo answered.

\*\*\*

Sheriff Lancaster received a call over his radio and nearly crapped himself at the description of the shit show taking place at the Rancho Grande Carniceria and Mercado. He requested backup and threw his empty onion ring container in a trashcan right outside his car window.

"Fuck, Cuervo. Make it a little more obvious you're up to shady shit! How the hell am I gonna explain more carnage?" he cursed, not realizing his ally and cash cow was already dead.

He turned on his lights and siren and sped out of the Burger Queen parking lot like a bat out of hell.

He hadn't even reached the shopping center parking lot before seeing the commotion. People were bleeding, women were crying, and cars were smashed into each other. He slowed down as a young man came running to his window.

"She went down the alley, over there beside the car wash!" he screamed.

"Hold on a goddamn minute, what the hell is going on here?" the sheriff asked.

"This bitch was on drugs or fucking possessed or some shit. She ran through the market tearing people up. Then she ran out here and started fuckin' shit up. People were trying to get away and crashing into other cars. It's a warzone here. I'd call for an ambulance and backup," the guy said, fishing his car keys out of his pocket.

"They're already on their way, boy. Are you hurt?"

"No, my mom got scratched and bitten, but she's okay because the bitch took off after someone threw a rosary at her. Crazy hoe thinks she's Dracula or some shit. I'm gonna find her and kill her ass after I take my mom to the hospital!"

"Hold on, that's my job. Anyone doing anything outside the law will be punished. I'm the man with the badge, and I say who dies. Help is on the way."

The guy scratched his head in frustration, then nodded. He knew he shouldn't have said anything about killing the psycho bitch in front of the sheriff, but he couldn't contain his anger.

"Have it your way, but I wouldn't get too cocky until you take a step inside the Rancho Grande."

The sheriff pulled his car closer to the front of the building and threw it in park.

"Y'all stand back," the sheriff shouted. "My boys are here and they're bringing an ambulance."

Patrol cars came screeching to a stop in the parking lot, and Sheriff Lancaster's men joined him for their instructions. He opened his mouth to speak, and a series of wails came from within the store. He feared the woman hadn't been working alone.

"Mendoza and Miller, head down the alley over there, we're looking for a deranged woman. She's dangerous, shoot to kill if you have to. Jacobs and Ashener, you're with me. Phillips and McDowell, you're on parking lot watch until this shit is sorted. Make sure the ambulances and EMTs are safe to tend to these folks. Let's move!"

The sheriff and his men moved swiftly into the Rancho Grande, weapons drawn. They walked in to a pool of blood and the store manager on his back, desperately trying to hold a hole in his throat closed. There was a cashier stretched over her grocery belt, her eyes wide but unblinking, half her face torn off and her cheekbone, jaw, and teeth visible.

"Motherfucker, what did this?" Ashener asked.

"Keep your guns up, gentlemen. We're not going down without a fight. Shoot to kill. I'm not interested in interrogations." His instructions were fueled by fear, half for the safety of his men, and half for his own political well-being. He couldn't afford for Cuervo's men to open their mouths about his partnership with their boss. He could only rationalize that the drug lord must have been pushing a new form of narcotic that drove people insane. The sheriff intended to put an end to it, but he also feared any links connecting him to allowing the drugs to be in the city to begin with.

A constant distraction of weeping and moaning drew his attention in all directions, but yelling guided him toward the back of the store. He got there in time to see a gang of demon-possessed cartel members writhing under a shower of table salt, and then Consuelo putting an end to them.

"What the fuck?" he murmured.

The old woman met his gaze as she wiped the end of the holy relic clean on her nightgown, like a warrior cleansing her blade of enemy blood. Two men stood with her; one he recognized as a rooster dealer for the cartels. The corpses of the men began to rot under the fluorescent lighting of the *mercado*, their skin flaking, their limbs shriveling. His mind went to the morgue and the bodies he had hauled in, all of whom had died under strange circumstances.

"Call Lisa! Right now!" he ordered over his shoulder.

"Yes, sir," Ashener said.

"What's going on here?" he asked, looking to Roy.

"You're probably not going to believe me if I tell you."

"Try me, asshole."

"These guys basically rose from the dead, and we had to kill them with a crucifix," Roy said.

"Does this have to do with the report of a deranged woman?" the sheriff asked.

"Yeah, everyone she kills is gonna end up coming back."

"WHAT?"

"Well, all hell is breaking loose here in Apache Wells," Roy said. "Literally."

# PANDEMONIUM

THE SHADOW MAN took a deep breath of night air. He could feel that Adriana was out there, shedding blood. Her power had grown since the night before, as he knew it would, and so had his. Chamuco would no longer be able to claim his body as his own. The drug lord would be a prisoner in his own mind, nothing more than a witness trapped in a flesh vehicle piloted by the ancient demon he'd allowed to take control. The taint Adriana was spreading was now at its apex, and anyone she killed would instantly become a member of the Shadow Man's army, a resident of his anti-utopia, Pandemonium. He looked up to the moon, a crimson ring glowing around its face, and he knew it was time.

\*\*\*

Consuelo, Roy, and Juan joined the sheriff and his men after securing the Rancho Grande. Officers were left with the paramedics as they started treating the victims left in Adriana's wake, and the hunt for Adriana began.

"How do we stop her?" Sheriff Lancaster asked.

"Only this will put an end to her killing," Consuelo said, lifting the large wooden crucifix.

"This really is some horror movie shit, you know that, right?" the sheriff said. "And these other bastards, the ones coming back to life, what do we do?"

"Arm your men with salt and crosses. They're not immortal...just strong." Consuelo spoke from experience, her mind plaguing her with momentary flashes from her past. A small town, its streets overrun with black-eyed demons, and she was one of them.

Roy recognized the heartbreaking remembrance in her eyes and put his hand on her shoulder. He, too, had done things in his life he wished he could change, but the cold hard truth was that they couldn't turn back time, only learn from it.

"Where will we get those on such short notice?"

Consuelo pointed back over her shoulder at the market. "There is plenty of salt in there, and things to make crosses with."

"Are they vampires?" Ashener asked.

"Not blood drinkers, soul eaters," Consuelo answered.

"How do you know all this? Are you the Latina Van Helsing?" the sheriff asked.

"Just shut up and do what she says," Roy fumed.

"You're right, we're losing time. Let's get this shit under control. Everyone step inside and arm yourself with bags of salt, and most importantly, a cross of some sort," Sheriff Lancaster said, and motioned to his men, and their army went to work making the only weaponry they knew that could do any good against the monsters Adriana was creating.

***

Mendoza drove the patrol car while Miller used a spotlight to illuminate the black alleyway through which the reportedly deranged woman had escaped. They had driven a few blocks down the alley, until it came to a dead end at a high fence. They caught a glimpse of movement, and Mendoza brought the car to a halt.

"Did you see that?"

"Yeah, she's down there. She's probably stuck back there where the fence borders the trailer park," Miller said.

"Sheriff Lancaster ordered shoot to kill, so get locked and loaded, buddy," Mendoza said.

Joseph Mendoza stepped out of the meager amount of safety provided by the vehicle and drew his weapon. A chill ran up his spine as he rounded the car to stand beside his partner, Henry Miller. There was no turning back now. They advanced toward a crunching sound that grew louder with every step they took down the alley. The beams of their flashlights cast a circle on a greasy set of dumpsters, and beyond them was a chain-link fence with a privacy screen attached to it. A soft whimpering amidst the crunching halted them. Mendoza felt his arm trembling, but he kept his pistol trained on the vicinity of the odd noises. Miller moved the beam of his flashlight downward, and a visible pool coming from the backside of the dumpster made him freeze. His concern grew to panic when a hand shot into view. It gripped the filthy side of the dumpster for a moment, then went limp. Miller glanced to Mendoza, who nodded back to him, and they slowly crept forward.

They rounded the dumpster and saw a woman sitting on a man's chest. His throat was torn open, and her mouth hovered just above the hole. She wasn't drinking his blood, but wisps of dark gray mist floated up out of the wound and into her waiting maw. The victim was an older homeless man Mendoza had arrested on a few occasions for drunk and disorderly conduct and pissing in a public space. Mendoza knew the man was dead by the way his blank eyes stared beyond him; the victim's life had left for good when he reached his hand out that final time and found no one to drag him away from the demon woman on his chest.

Miller pulled the trigger first. His bullet grazed the side of Adriana's head and tore off the top of her ear. She hissed and rolled off her prey. She was on her feet and coming at them in a matter of seconds, her movement so fast it only registered as a blur of shadow and teeth to the two sheriff's deputies. She grabbed Mendoza by the throat and crushed his windpipe in a single squeeze, then tore it free, his blood showering her face. She dropped him lifeless to the dirty ground and went for his partner. Miller dove out of her way and rolled. He got to his feet and fired his gun wildly, but didn't manage to hit her again. Adriana shot out of the shadows and punched her fist into his stomach. It stopped him immediately and stole his breath. Miller stared at her, agony burrowing further into him as she forced her fist upward and grabbed hold of any soft tissue she could. Adriana ripped her fist free and brought a handful of bleeding meat to her mouth, which she lapped at while watching the life leave his wide, terrified eyes. Adriana knelt over him and coaxed his soul into her hungry mouth.

She leaped up to perch on the top of the tall chain-link fence. With each feeding she grew more powerful, more nimble. Her black eyes scanned the trailer park, and her ears focused on the sounds of humanity alive within it. It made her stomach growl and her heart race at the thought of how many souls were there, all just waiting in thin metal packages. The trailers were like lunchboxes to the soul eater. She would rip them open and feast on the morsels inside.

Deputy Tina Rover halted behind the patrol cruiser. She noted the driver's side and passenger side doors were hanging open, as if the occupants had planned on coming right back. She exited her car and waited for her partner, Stephen Carry, to join her. They both kept quiet and used hand motions to signal to one another as they headed down the alleyway. They only got a few yards when Tina's flashlight spilled over Deputy Miller's body lying on the pavement. Not far from him lay

Mendoza, and peeking out from behind the dumpster was a pale hand. The fence beyond the dumpster rattled, and a shadow sat atop it like an oversized bird on a precarious roost. Deputy Carry pointed his flashlight at the shadow to reveal a woman with completely black eyes.

"She's a fuckin' demon," he said.

"Radio it in," Deputy Rover whispered to Deputy Carry, her arm shaking as she kept her pistol trained on the shadow.

He gripped the radio suspended from his shoulder and attempted to radio Sheriff Lancaster their location, their discovery of two dead deputies, and how they possibly had the suspect cornered. Instead, Deputy Carry's voice came hysterically across the radio, followed by frantic gunfire, then silence.

***

Sheriff Lancaster screamed in frustration. "This fuckin' bitch has to pay. Let's go!"

His small group was armed with all they could find in the market, and he was done fucking around. He wanted Adriana dead for her crimes; whether her grandmother felt the same, he didn't care.

***

Deputy Carry watched in disappointment as the deranged woman jumped from the top of the fence to the other side, toward the trailer park, and disappeared. His partner cursed and lowered her weapon, but as she spun to check on the fallen deputies, she was tackled. He pointed his gun at her attacker and hesitated in disbelief—she was being assaulted by the very deputy they'd reported as dead. He pulled the trigger, and his bullet passed through the side of the dead deputy's gaping neck. The dead man paid no attention to the wound as his hands found Deputy Rover's screaming mouth. He gripped her top and bottom jaw and pried them apart until her mouth hung open at an agonizing angle. Tears ran down her cheeks as her voice became a ragged cry. She scrambled until her hand found her own gun, then fired once into the chest of the demon deputy, but he just plunged his fist down her throat, deeper and deeper, until she stopped struggling.

Her partner ran, casting aside his bravery in favor of survival. He could see the patrol cruiser with its doors open, and it called to him like a beacon. He pushed himself to run faster, but he could hear the wheezing exhalations of one of the creatures behind him as it pursued him. Desperate tears ran down his face and his chest felt as if it would burst, but he kept forcing himself forward. He didn't want to die. He didn't want his jaws forced apart. His feet pounded the pavement. His eyes were fixed on the car, his salvation. Other patrol cars arrived; they parked next to his cruiser and the other empty one that his dead companions had left behind. His tears became those of joy and hope as he ran toward the sheriff, whose face looked determined and angry.

Sheriff Lancaster watched the young deputy's face transform from hope to unbelievable despair when hands found his shoulders. His body tumbled forward, and the demon attacking him went with him. They rolled to the pavement so hard that the sheriff could hear Deputy Carry's wrists snap on impact. The monster on his back was dressed in a deputy's uniform; it was once one of his comrades. Sheriff Lancaster drew his pistol and blasted a wide hole in the demon's forehead, but it just rocked back and then continued its attack on Deputy Carry, clawing at the back of his head until its fingers carved a hole. It ripped upward and took a massive piece of the young deputy's scalp away.

"Wait!"

Consuelo screamed and ran towards the demon. She threw a handful of salt in its black eyes and it fell off its victim's back. She raised her crucifix and let it fall into its throat. A muffled hiss came from the wound, and the demon collapsed.

"Thank you!" Deputy Carry wept. His missing scalp felt like his head was doused in gasoline and set on fire, but the relief he felt at the death of the demon overshadowed it.

Sheriff Lancaster joined Consuelo, as did Roy and Juan. The sheriff nodded toward the dark end of the alley and the dumpster. "That wasn't the only black-eyed bastard."

"Let's put these motherfuckers down," Roy said.

They were met by what used to be Deputy Mendoza and Deputy Rover. The two were still locked in a dance of death as Mendoza buried his face in her gaping mouth. It looked like a monstrous make-out session was in progress, but Consuelo knew he was swallowing her soul, and once it was gone she, too, would re-awaken and ravenously seek the souls of the living. Consuelo lifted a container of salt and said a prayer. The beast turned its eyes to her, and she let the salt fly. It burned holes into the beast and released the body of Deputy Rover. It leaped at her as she lifted the crucifix, knocking it from her hand. She tumbled beneath the demon and landed with it sitting on her chest. Her salt had been lost in the fall too, leaving her defenseless. The demon's breath smelled of decay, and she knew its insides would already be black and putrefied. A gunshot sent the demon tumbling sideways. The sheriff wasn't letting Consuelo go down so easily.

"Kill the sonofabitch!" he cried.

Juan ran forward and emptied an aluminum canister of salt onto the demon's head. It screeched and writhed. He lifted a cross he had constructed from a broken broom handle and duct tape. The demon swiped feebly at the crude crucifix, but its strength had waned enough for Juan to plunge the cross into the demon's chest. Deputy Rover was beginning to squirm with undead life, but Roy tore open a bag of salt and dumped it on her. Her mouth gaped open with unhinged jaws, like a disfigured snake. She shrieked, rolled over, and tried to crawl away, but he pressed his foot into her back, then drove a homemade cross into her. She clawed at the pavement and tried reaching back to dislodge the weapon, so Roy pulled it out and drove it into her over and over until she finally lay still. The dead homeless man then made his attack, but Consuelo was already back on her feet, crucifix in hand and ready for him. Salt ate holes into his eyes and he stumbled back, leaving his chest open for her killing blow. The crucifix slid into his flesh easily, and penetrated his already decaying heart. He fell back against the dumpster and left a trail of black blood in the dumpster juices decorating its rusty side as he slid to the ground.

Juan pulled a fifth of whiskey out of his pocket; he had "borrowed" it from the *mercado* when they were readying themselves for battle.

"Let me hit that shit," Roy said.

The sheriff reached his hand out too. "Pass it this way, boy."

They took a moment to ply their bodies with the strong, warm liquor and devise a hasty plan before they went back to the cruisers. They would split up for the time being in order to put down the groups of demons they knew would be multiplying as Adriana killed more and more.

"You wanna ride with me?" the sheriff asked Juan, noticeably eyeing Juan's whiskey bottle.

"Sure," Juan answered.

"Help me out with the injured deputy," he said, and they assisted Deputy Carry into the back of the cruiser.

The sheriff then turned to Roy and Consuelo. "All right, you two can take that cruiser, and we'll head back out there. My men, as limited as they are, are armed with the same shit we got. They should be putting some of these bastards down, so let's join them."

"We need to find Adriana, that will end all of this," Consuelo said.

Sheriff Lancaster nodded. "Get to it, and good luck."

Juan climbed into the passenger seat, and Sheriff Lancaster already had his hand stuck out. "Pass me more liquid courage."

"We have to warn everyone, the people don't know..." Deputy Carry said from the backseat.

Juan handed the sheriff the bottle, and he took a big swig as he contemplated his decisions.

"I only have one option to try to stem the growth of these bastards, give us a fighting chance," the sheriff said.

Sheriff Lancaster brought his radio to his lips and ordered the station to alert the news. Apache Wells would be put into lockdown. He ordered his deputies to force all civilians to return to their homes and stay put. He wasn't worried about the mayor's reaction. That old man, who was probably fast asleep in the arms of a call girl, would have no choice but to keep his people off the streets in the sudden dire emergency they faced. They would be nothing but lambs brought to a slaughter if they encountered any of demonic corpses left in Adriana's path.

"How can we kill these things?" Deputy Carry asked.

"Only holy things work. And salt hurts them, but it doesn't kill them," Juan said.

"That's why our guns didn't do shit," the deputy said, his voice shaking.

Juan knew the poor guy had just been through a nightmare, so he passed his bottle back over the seat. The injured deputy accepted it gratefully and took a big swallow.

Sheriff Lancaster jerked his head in Juan's direction and smiled. "I think I know how to make our bullets worth a shit again!"

"I don't know what you got in mind, but I hope it fucking works," Deputy Carry said.

They sped away and Roy watched them from behind the wheel of the cruiser that had been left behind by Deputies Mendoza and Miller.

# DEMON MOTHERFUCKERS

"IF SHE WAS back here, the only escape was over the fence. She's in the trailer park," Roy said grimly.

His mind strayed to how many families lived there, all of his neighbors and their kids. He felt a cold dagger of fear run through him. He didn't want to see Adriana wreak havoc in the small community; it would be a nightmare.

The streets had a strong presence of sheriff's deputies. They were instructed to alert people to return to their homes, while keeping an eye out for any suspicious activities. Many of the people of Apache Wells followed the directive, but there was still a group who didn't. They refused to follow any orders put out by the sheriff, which unknowingly left them open to becoming members of the Shadow Man's undead army.

Lisa and Minnie stumbled from the coroner's office, their eyes black and their stomachs rumbling for a taste of the living. Behind them came the group of dead men, Ritchie and the vagrants, lurching along with their abdomens still hanging open from their examinations on Lisa's cold steel tables. They preyed upon those who refused to follow Sheriff Lancaster's orders, causing a ripple effect as those new victims became possessed, then in turn attacked other people and left them with the undead hunger. Car alarms wailed in the streets, people screamed, and death came to greet them in the form of unrelenting, black-eyed gangs.

"My children," the Shadow Man said, as they drove past the hordes in Gusano's black hearse.

The Shadow Man and the three Gusanos weren't concerned with the local law enforcement; they just kept following the internal call Adriana produced. It was like a heartbeat drawing them closer to her. The *brujo* drove his hearse down the dark streets, while his master and the twins focused on Adriana. The Gusanos weren't as strong as their master, but they were imbued with certain powers for their undying loyalty. They were a step above the ordinary demons awakening from death, hungry for souls, but they were still not immortal or as gifted as Adriana had become in just twenty-four hours. They were meant to be fierce servants of the

Shadow Man and whatever bride he chose to sit beside him as he ruled over Pandemonium.

"She is near. I feel her devouring many souls. My queen will be unstoppable." The Shadow Man was pleased.

He pointed to the sky beyond the windshield; the red ring around the moon had a fiery glow.

"The doorway is ready."

# THE LADY OUTSIDE

AUBREY WAS MAKING a mud pie in her backyard under the porch light. Her mother was inside on the phone arguing with who the girl could only guess was her daddy, Chuck. Her mama always fought with him. The girl could hear her through an open window; her voice was nearly a growl, and it made young Aubrey flinch. Whenever her mom talked like a snarling dog, with her teeth clenched and her lips curled back, it meant she was about to say something ugly. When she said the really bad stuff to Aubrey, she would usually apologize later and buy the girl a treat from the ice cream truck that rolled through the trailer park every evening, but her mama never apologized to her father. Instead she would stomp through the kitchen and throw her phone into the living room; she'd call him a fucking bastard and other bad words. The girl couldn't remember a time her mother wasn't yelling at a phone in all her ten years of life. It made Aubrey's eyes water, little tears hanging momentarily from her long eyelashes before falling onto her mud pie.

"Hey, Aubrey." A small whisper hailed her from the falling darkness.

Terrence stepped out of his hiding spot, and she smiled a small grin. He was her best friend around the park. He was a few years younger than her, but he was tall and didn't let any of the other boys call her names.

"Hey, Terry!"

"Is your mom being mean to your dad again?" He cocked his head toward the loud voice coming from the window.

"Yeah, like always."

"You wanna play?" he asked.

"I don't know…"

"Come on, it'll make you feel better."

"Okay, but it's getting dark, so we got to stay in my yard or my mom will kill me."

"Okay. I brought my slingshot. Wanna set up cans and knock 'em down?"

Aubrey agreed and led Terrence around the side of the trailer, where her mother kept aluminum cans to be exchanged for money. She grabbed

two twenty-four-ounce beer cans and two soda pop cans, and they went to
the back yard. The fences between the yards weren't very high, but the one
along the back edge of her small plot of land was about her height, so they
turned the cans upside down and jammed the twisted tops of the chain-
link fence into the cans' drinking holes. Aubrey usually just played with
her dolls and pretended to cook, but Terrence always taught her stuff boys
liked to play, rough things her mother would disapprove of like building
ramps for bicycles and jumping over them, building tree houses, and
shooting his slingshot. She didn't know why her mama made a big deal
out of silly things; kids could play whatever they liked, but her mother
always told her she was a girl and could only play girly things.

Aubrey felt a jolt of excitement as she scooped up a rock. She didn't
care if her mama caught her and called her names; Aubrey would tell her
to stick her ice cream cone where the sun didn't shine. She loaded her
rock in the slingshot and drew it back, taking aim at one of the beer cans.
She let the rock fly, and it hit its target with a loud metallic ding. Aubrey
handed the slingshot over to Terrence, who high-fived her and then took
position to try his luck hitting the cans in the dark.

"AUBREY!"

The shrill voice caused Terrence to jump. He let loose his rock and it
sailed beyond its target, but he no longer cared whether he hit the can or
not. Aubrey was about to be in trouble, and it was all his fault.

"I fuckin' told you not to play like that. You're a girl, not a damn
truck driver!"

Aubrey's mother was a thin woman, so thin her knees looked like
doorknobs on sticks beneath her pale skin, but her hand was rock hard
when she slapped the girl. Terrence stepped between Aubrey and her
mother, Jennifer.

"I was just showing her I got better at aiming. She didn't do
anything."

"Get outta the way, little boy."

"Mama, he's telling the truth," Aubrey lied, and she hoped the dark
would conceal the guilt in her eyes.

Jennifer paused, her hands on her hips. "You better not be lying."

"I swear, I'm not, mama. I was just watching."

Her bony mother grabbed Terrence by his arm, and he squealed at
her sharp nails biting into his skin. "Go home."

Terrence nodded and tried to yank his arm away, but her grip was too
strong. He wanted to cuss her out, but he decided he'd let his mom do

that. Aubrey's mom had no idea the hell she would go through once he got home and told his mama and his older sister. The bony bitch would be begging for mercy when they were through with her.

A flash of movement behind Jennifer caught Aubrey's attention. Something had dashed behind her mother through the darkness of their back yard, but Jennifer was too busy focusing her angry eyes on Terrence to notice. The blur of a figure, moving incredibly fast, flashed by again. Whoever or whatever it was went dashing between the black shadows of the old mulberry trees she liked to have picnics by with her baby dolls.

"Mommy..."

"Shut your mouth!" her mother ordered as she continued to squeeze Terrence's arm, her gaze like Medusa's turning him to a statue of fear.

Aubrey stumbled back when the blurred figure halted behind her mother. It was a woman, and her eyes were black. Jennifer's head snapped back, and she released Terrence. The black-eyed woman had her by the hair. Terrence turned and screamed as the woman snapped Aubrey's mother's neck and blood shot from between her thin lips.

***

Tanya lived behind Aubrey. They played together sometimes, but usually she was scared of Aubrey's mama, so she stayed in her own yard. Tanya could hear Aubrey's mom yelling again; she was always yelling. She was a scary lady, and Tanya felt really bad for Aubrey. Sometimes she wished Aubrey could come live with her and her grandma and grandpa; then her friend would be happy all the time, just like she was. Her grandparents had always taken good care of Tanya, always bought her toys and cookies, and always hugged her each night before bed. Her grandma was sitting in the living room, watching a game show like she always did before heading off to bed, while Tanya sat by her window daydreaming about saving Aubrey from her mean old mama. She was watching out her tiny bedroom window as Aubrey sat by her porch in the light of the falling sun until it went dark and Terrence came to play. She grew excited when she saw them hanging cans from the back fence; she knew that meant Terry had brought over the slingshot Santa brought him for Christmas. She had tried the slingshot once, though her arms weren't strong enough to pull it back yet, but Terrence had been nice and reassured her that when she got a little bigger, she could fire one too.

She watched them in the near darkness with a mixture of wonder and fear. The happiness they radiated when they played was only dimmed by the looming threat of Aubrey's mean mama. Where they stood there was really no light, but the glow of the porch lights in all the yards illuminated them enough to show they were having a great time. When the skinny woman came marching out the back door, Tanya held her breath and fretted, knowing her friends were in big trouble. She watched as Aubrey's mom grabbed Terrence by the arm, and even in the dark she could tell by the way his body tensed that Aubrey's mom was hurting him. Tanya sprang from her bed; she would tell her grandma and grandpa, she knew they wouldn't allow Aubrey's mama to hurt Terrence. They would yell at her and make her let him go.

But as Tanya tried to peel her attention away from the scene in Aubrey's yard, her eyes caught a dashing movement. It came so quickly, she blinked and suddenly there stood a woman in the dark. The woman had black eyes, and she held Aubrey's mom by the hair. In a quick motion, the lady twisted Aubrey's mom's neck, and Tanya watched blood fly from her mouth.

Tanya ran from her room screaming, startling her grandparents, who were half-asleep on the couch while *Wheel of Fortune* played on the TV.

"Help! Help!"

"What's going on?" her grandma asked.

"The lady outside... She's gonna hurt Aubrey!"

# BAPTIZED BULLETS

SHERIFF LANCASTER SPED down the street, not very cautious of who stepped in the path of his vehicle. There were groups of demon-possessed citizens already gathering, clawing at windows and wreaking havoc on any humans they came in contact with. He knew the situation was growing out of control by the second—many of the people of Apache Wells wouldn't abide by the order to stay indoors, and some couldn't possibly make it home in time to avoid being attacked. They would find out only once it was too late that Apache Wells was becoming Hell on Earth. His destination wasn't far now—he took a left and, in the middle of a side street, a familiar pair stood over a man gripping a wound in his throat. The sheriff knew them instantly, but their eyes gave them away; they had already been changed. Lisa and Minnie were illuminated by his headlights, and with them were the same corpses he'd had his men haul to the coroner's office.

"My God," he said. His gut twisted, and he looked to Juan.

"Run them over," Juan said.

"Do it!" the wounded deputy in the backseat urged.

The two women came for them, leaping onto the hood of the car and beating the windshield with their bloody fists. Sheriff Lancaster hit the gas, and they rolled from the hood and away from the car. The group of demonic corpses stood firm, but they were no match for three thousand-plus pounds of steel. He held the gas pedal to the floor and left them screeching on the blacktop, some half-run over but still clinging to their horrific new existence.

"Where are we going?" Juan asked, his anxiety screaming for an answer.

"We're here," Sheriff Lancaster said as he turned the wheel and the cruiser fishtailed into a church parking lot.

Juan grinned and crossed himself. "*Gracias a dios.*"

"Now you're probably figuring out my plan."

"Yes, let's go!" Juan said.

"Don't leave me here," Deputy Carry pleaded from the backseat.

"I didn't plan on it," the sheriff answered. "Get your ass ready to run."

A handful of other patrol cars joined them, and they climbed from the limited safety they felt in the cruiser. Juan assisted Deputy Carry as the sheriff motioned his men into the church.

"Find the holy water, baptize your damn bullets, and grab anything else with a cross on it." His eyes fell beyond the parking lot to a group of staggering figures. One stepped beneath a streetlight—it was Lisa, and she'd brought a small army with her.

"The bitch followed us," Sheriff Lancaster cursed. "MOVE!"

They had almost made it to the long stairway leading to the church doors, but a group of black-eyed teenagers stopped them. A girl in a red tank top leaped on Sheriff Lancaster, her teeth snapping inches from his nose. Juan grabbed her by her hair and yanked her to the ground, then drove his homemade cross into her chest. She wailed as black blood flew from her gaping mouth and she died. The other two teens grabbed one of Sheriff Lancaster's men, and nearly yanked his arms from their sockets before the other deputies fell on them with nightsticks. Sickeningly the demons continued to fight for their meal, even as all their bones were broken and their limbs were rendered useless. They writhed on the ground until Juan brought his cross over and drove it deep into them, leaving them moving and screeching no more.

Sheriff Lancaster grabbed Juan by the shoulder. "Let's go, they're coming."

He pointed to Lisa and Minnie, who were creeping quickly along in the shadows of the trees in an attempt to catch them before they made it into the holy sanctuary.

The sheriff and his men hurried up the church steps and pushed the heavy wooden doors open. He recalled the priest, Guillermo, who used to take such good care of the old church. He liked to keep the doors open for anyone seeking refuge from the world outside. His wisdom would have been invaluable now, but he was gone, his body and head separated. His head had never been found. Sheriff Lancaster tried to banish the memory of finding Padre Guillermo's corpse, dusty and blood-drained, his skin gray and lifeless. The sheriff knew his death was linked to more than just a cartel feud; Padre Guillermo was the enemy of the evil taking over Apache Wells. It hurt Sheriff Lancaster's heart to think of how kind the priest was, and how his death affected the entire community, but as he made his way into the church, he swore he heard the voice of the departed holy man. His soul was still there, speaking the words of God and reveling in the heavenly sanctuary of the old church; he would assure that their bullets became holy weaponry. Sheriff Lancaster came to stand before the white stone altar; on the wall behind it hung a large golden crucifix. The sheriff walked reverently to it and ran his fingertips over it. He felt a quickening of his heartbeat.

"Mind if I borrow this, Padre?"

He gripped it and lifted it gently off the wall, then held it firmly in his palm. For a moment he felt unworthy of it, as if he wasn't the one who should wield it, not after the life he had led. He clutched it against his chest and turned to the voices of his men as they searched for the holy water in the darkness.

"Over here!" one of his deputies called.

They gathered around the small fountain-like stoup filled with the crystal-clear water Padre Guillermo had blessed. It had a cross hanging above it, and to the right was a large stained-glass window. The sheriff looked out at the gathering of shadows; they didn't advance beyond the parking lot. He knew they had to be held at bay by the power of this holy place, which gave him an idea.

"Cloones," he said to one of his deputies, "once we get outta here, I want you and Kramer to get the word out to anyone looking for a safe place. This is it. Provide them with protection until they get here. Keep doing that until..."

"Until?"

"Well, until you know if we succeed or not."

"You got it."

"Deputy Carry, stay here and welcome people in who need help."

"I can still fight, I wanna fight..."

"Those are my orders."

The deputy nodded, accepting Sheriff Lancaster's instructions.

"The rest of you, get your rounds baptized in this holy water and let's get going."

Juan dipped his broomstick cross in the sacred water, and the sheriff scoffed. "Give this man a gun!"

\*\*\*

They strode from the church, hands still wet with holy water. The sheriff held the golden cross out before him, and his men followed behind with their weapons ready. The group of demonic dead turned their attention to the approaching humans and hissed at the sheriff. They were crawling and perching on the patrol cars, waiting to devour the group emerging from the church. Their dark eyes fell on Lancaster hungrily, but the holy relic in his hand sent them scurrying back. They clawed at the air and drooled, their ravenous hunger for souls demanding they attack.

"Come get it, you ugly motherfuckers!"

Lisa's jaws hung open like a demon python, ready to swallow him whole.

"You were a decent woman. I'm sorry it ended up like this," Sheriff Lancaster said.

He drew his pistol and put a holy bullet in her right eye. Minnie was beside her, emotionless when Lisa was put down. She lifted her hand and clawed the air with broken, bloody nails. Her lips were violet and cracked, her tongue black. She gnashed her teeth and ran for him. Juan shot from his hip, blasting the side of Minnie's head off. She tumbled and fell to the ground, the massive wound leaking a pool of dark blood at their feet.

"That's what I like to see. Let's blast these bastards!" the sheriff cried.

His men fanned out, causing some of the demons to leap forward impatiently. They opened fire, their bullets burning through demon flesh like a knife through warm butter. Dark blood rained down on Sheriff Lancaster and Juan as they cut them down. It was only a handful of minutes, but it felt like an eternity of wailing, clawing, bullets, and blood. They kicked the corpses aside and made their way to their cars.

A crackling voice over the radio reminded Juan of where the next battle would be.

"Roy needs backup," Juan said.

Sheriff Lancaster lifted the radio, his face set in a confident grin.

# CRUCIFIXES AND ROOSTER POWDER

ROY AND CONSUELO drove through the front gate of the trailer park to find that chaos was already rampant. Consuelo pointed to the front yard of a woman Roy knew for years, a seventy year old former flight attendant by the name of Sherrie.

"There she is," the *curandera* said.

Roy could see Adriana twisting Sherrie's head around on her limp neck, and around her stood a wild group of mangled men, women, and children, their eyes black and hungry.

He lifted the radio in the car and brought it to his lips, hoping he could catch the sheriff and Juan still among the living. "Sheriff Lancaster, we have located Adriana. She's in the Western Winds trailer park."

"We're reloading and will be right over."

Roy placed the radio down on the dash and glanced over to Consuelo, who stared out at the sky. Her face was a mask of cold fear as her eyes fixed on the moon. It was ringed in fire.

The radio went wild with the sheriff ordering his men to gather at his location, and Roy recognized the address: it was the church. He prayed the sheriff had a trick up his sleeve, because in only a few minutes the horde created by Adriana was growing, and he wasn't confident he and Consuelo could handle them.

"Can we stop her?" he asked.

"We don't have a choice," Consuelo answered.

"You've lived through this before, haven't you?" he asked.

Consuelo turned to him and he could see through her pale nightgown the lines of blood tracing down her body. "My wounds are open again. They will never heal from the last time I fought him. I don't want Adriana to feel this pain, this fear."

"Can we save her?"

"We can and will, but she will never be the same," Consuelo answered sadly. She steadied herself and gripped the handle of the car door. "But as long as she's alive, then she will never be his. Not in this life or any other. Let's go."

Roy armed himself with all they had, salt and a homemade cross Juan had taped together for him out of a broom handle. He didn't know what Sheriff Lancaster meant by reloading, but he hoped it would be enough to end the growing army of demonic corpses. He got out of the car as silently as he could, took a deep breath, and strode forward.

The crowd of demons gathering on the lawn grew as they advanced toward them, but none of them was aware of the *curandera* and her partner. Roy pushed aside the fact that he knew these people in life; they were dead now, and would stop at nothing to kill him and Consuelo. They breached the glow of the street light, and Adriana turned her eyes to them. Her army spun around at her shrieking, wordless command. A group of at least twenty with snarling, drooling mouths stared at the two humans hungrily, but awaited Adriana's orders.

Consuelo gripped her sack of salt and her crucifix and took a deep breath before pulling Roy closer to her. The stillness of the night was broken in an instant as Adriana uttered a guttural grunt. The horde leaped forward, ready to kill. The old woman spun in a circle and laid out a barrier of salt on the ground around her and Roy. The demons came to a crashing halt at the rough white line and pawed at the air before them. Consuelo began tossing handfuls of salt on them, and they retreated with screeching wails of pain. They stopped only feet away. The hunger in their guts hurt more than the temporary burning the salt invoked; it was a hollow agony that wouldn't abate unless they found a way to get their teeth into the humans hiding in the salt circle. A child-demon grew too impatient and ran for them. It jumped into the air and fell, tumbling like a dead bird from the sky when it crossed the sacred circle at their feet. Consuelo drove the end of her crucifix into its delicate chest and whispered a prayer over it mercifully.

The loud blast of a horn made Roy and Consuelo spin around, hoping the sheriff had come with his men. Their hopes were crushed when they saw a big black hearse. It was the same one they'd watched El Gusano climb out of at the truck stop after Wanda's exorcism. Consuelo wished she had never accepted his help. He'd revealed himself as a rat in league with her greatest foe, but at the time she'd thought of him only as a two-bit *brujo* whose actual job was making corpses disappear. If she had only known he was a bloodhound who already had her scent in its snout, and had conned a power hungry *narco* into unleashing *El Hombre Sombra* into the world again, she would have battled him right then and there and spared Adriana the nightmare of becoming the Shadow Man's bride.

*Los Tres Gusanos* exited the vehicle, and behind them came a man dressed in a black velvet suit. Consuelo's breath caught in her throat at the sight of him. His flesh bore no sign of Chamuco anymore. His change was complete. He wore the same human disguise he had many years before, a handsome man with long dark hair and the smile of a wolf. She brought her hand up to her chest and felt the old wounds yawn open, warm blood spilling from them.

"Black eyes," the Shadow Man said, "time has not been kind to you. I, on the other hand, am eternal. You could have been too, but I guess your granddaughter will do."

"*Hijo de puta,*" she cursed.

"Always a fierce one, that's what I liked about you. You definitely put up more of a fight than young Adriana, but I guess I didn't give her a choice."

He walked a wide circle around Consuelo and Roy, avoiding the line of salt. Adriana came to him as he lifted his hand and beckoned her over. Her submissiveness twisted Consuelo's gut: not because she was ashamed of her granddaughter, but because she too had once been like a lapdog to him. Consuelo still couldn't outrun the shame she felt at becoming one of his creatures, and now, seeing her granddaughter walking the same path made her physically ill.

"How much do you think you can bleed and still be strong enough to fight me?" he asked Consuelo.

El Gusano and the twin *brujas* laughed, their voices like jackals in the darkness.

Consuelo's body trembled, and she felt herself growing cold and weak.

"She isn't alone!" Roy said, and threw a handful of salt directly on *El Hombre Sombra* and his servants.

They fell back, skin bubbling, mouths falling open in angry cries. Roy scooped Consuelo up in his arms, and they ran for the cruiser. He struggled to open the door and place her inside. He felt a bulge in his pocket and remembered the rooster powder he'd taken from Hector's corpse. He shook the red bag out on the old woman and closed the car door. He turned with the black bag to face his enemy. The Shadow Man had the face of a monster when he was angry, revealing his true demonic visage. He slashed his claws at Roy, who jumped back, pulled the black bag open, and tossed it on *El Hombre Sombra* as he fell on him. He clung to Roy and bit into the side of his neck, then coughed and fell away, affected by the black magic, but only for a moment. He got to his feet and came for Roy again, who began dusting himself with salt. The Shadow Man fell away from him, but laughed. "You can't kill me with salt and spells."

"Yeah, but they burn, don't they, you bastard?"

*El Hombre Sombra* growled in rage at the human's defiance. Soon, Roy was completely surrounded by the black-eyed demons. They came to kill him and appease their master. The Shadow Man ordered them back and held his hand out to Adriana. She came to his side obediently. There were gunshots in the distance, and he laughed. "Humans always try to resist. If they just accepted this new world, it would go much easier for them."

"We don't want your new world, asshole," Roy said.

"Feed on him," the Shadow Man ordered Adriana.

"Stop! Don't you remember me?" Roy said.

"She's no longer in there. She is my servant. She will do as I tell her just as they all do!"

Roy looked around him. The demons all stood back at their master's command. The Shadow Man was feeding Roy to Adriana just to demonstrate his complete control. Roy felt hopeless, like a rabbit in the jaws of a coyote.

"Do it!" the Shadow Man said.

Adriana lunged at Roy, and they tumbled back against the sheriff's cruiser. Her strength was unimaginable as she gripped the sides of his head and brought her mouth toward his throat. She meant to bite into him like an apple. Roy lifted his hands and placed them on her throat, then squeezed while pushing her backwards. It was futile, and he knew it. Adriana's breath was hot and smelled like an open grave, and her teeth snapped only inches from his flesh.

A sudden horn blast distracted Adriana and all those watching and waiting for her to shed his blood. Several sheriff's cruisers came flying into the driveway of the trailer park, and over the loud-speaker Sheriff Lancaster spoke: "We've come to send you back to Hell!"

He and his men exited their vehicles, pistols and rifles drawn. The sheriff had the swagger of a man who knew he was on the verge of victory.

"Let him go, demon bitch!"

"You stupid man. You can't kill us with bullets!" The Shadow Man laughed.

"Maybe not ordinary bullets, but bullets bathed in holy water...I think those will fuck your day up!"

The sheriff opened fire. Juan and his men followed his lead, and he was right. The bullets penetrated the demons' flesh and blasted white-hot holes through them. Their flesh sizzled and smoked, and they fell lifeless to the ground. Juan shot at the twin *brujas* who stood protectively in front of their master, splitting their heads open and sending pieces of their brains onto El Gusano. The *brujo* pushed *El Hombre Sombra* and Adriana away like a bodyguard, and they fled for the hearse. A bullet caught Adriana's shoulder, and she spun and fell to the ground. El Gusano kept running, but his master stopped and turned to pick Adriana up. The sheriff lifted his pistol, took aim, and blasted a hole through the monstrous *brujo*'s skull.

"Where's your army now?" Roy asked.

"I don't need an army to open the door. Look at it." the Shadow Man said, and pointed to the sky.

The ring around the moon had grown bigger, its flames bright, and beyond them a swirling darkness was slowly spinning.

"Come, my dear. Play time is over. It's time to speak the magic words and call open the door."

"I'm gonna kill her, then," the sheriff said.

"NO!" the old woman cried.

Juan grabbed the sheriff's gun, and he looked to Consuelo, who had climbed out of the car. Her injuries had ceased bleeding. The rooster powder had sealed her wounds from long ago once more and left her with new strength. She carried the crucifix and a bag of salt.

"The door is already opening, and the only way to stop this is to kill the source of the evil," Consuelo said. "On my orders, Sheriff."

Consuelo rushed toward the Shadow Man and Adriana. She lifted the bag of salt and tossed its contents onto her granddaughter. The possessed young woman shrieked and fell away as it ate into her skin. The Shadow Man gripped Adriana's hand but couldn't shield himself from Consuelo, who brought the crucifix up and then jammed it downward into his chest. He released Adriana and grabbed Consuelo by the hair. His strength was waning, but was still too much for the old *curandera*. The spinning circle above them became a vacuum, sucking them both into it.

They struggled against one another as they were lifted up. The *curandera* forced the crucifix deeper into him and then screamed, "NOW!"

The sheriff and his men opened fire; their blessed bullets blew holes in the Shadow Man's human form. Sunrise was nearing, and the moon was slowly retreating. He wouldn't be able to be anything more than an entity again soon, a spirit waiting for someone foolish enough to allow him into their body. His dream of unleashing Pandemonium was shattered again, and he knew it. With his dying hands, he twisted Consuelo's head around on her neck. The doorway sucked them into darkness and closed in the blink of an eye.

"I'll see you again, black-eyes!" his voice screeched from beyond the dark sky.

The demonic corpses fell to the ground, dead once more, and the ring of fire in the sky was nowhere to be seen.

"We beat the son of a bitch!" Sheriff Lancaster cried.

Roy went to Adriana, who was barely breathing. Her body was hers again, completely human, and the many wounds she'd sustained left her clinging to life. She opened her dark eyes and stared up at Roy. He held her hand and waited for an ambulance to come.

"I can't believe she's gone," Juan said as he approached them, his eyes fixed on the sky above him.

"Yes, but never forgotten. She will live on in Adriana."

# THE HIGHWAY

THE THREE FRIENDS sat on the tailgate of Juan's truck. It was daylight, so the truck stop's new pimp didn't attempt to sell them any company. Adriana brought a bottle to her lips and took a big swig. The liquor burned her insides, but she smiled and passed it to Roy.

"Just one, I gotta drive!" he laughed, and took a drink.

Juan took his bottle back and waited, watching the highway. "Is he coming or not?"

"He's always late, or drunk, or sleeping," Adriana said.

"There's the bastard." Roy pointed out the sheriff's car barreling toward them from the long stretch of dusty highway.

He parked beside them and got out with a shit-eating grin.

"What did you have to offer us?" Juan asked.

"Today was supposed to be the big cockfight, but that obviously didn't happen."

"Yeah, I guess not." Juan laughed.

"I have two groups without leaders," he said, and took Juan's whiskey, raised it to the three as a toast, then continued. "They need someone to whip them into shape, and the bosses want them to be combined into a single cartel again. I obviously can't do it, since I'm a public figure, but how about you, Juan?" He took a drink and handed it back.

"Me? What do you mean?"

"The drug operation, dipshit."

"You want me to take over as a drug lord?" Juan asked.

"Yeah. I've been in contact with my partners in Mexico, and they gave me the okay to choose someone trustworthy. Who better than the man I fought demons with?"

"They don't want to choose for themselves?" Roy asked.

"Oh, hell no. They trust me, and can't do it without my support. I've been helping them run drugs through here for more than twenty years, so they gave me my choice of associates. I need someone who knows the area, speaks the gringo tongue, and is willing to follow orders."

Juan smiled. "Are you serious?"

"You bet your ass I'm serious, but I get to renegotiate my cut."

"Of course you do, you bastard!" Juan smiled.

"Well, what do you say?"

"You have a deal," Juan said.

"And you two, are you still leaving?" the sheriff asked.

Roy and Adriana nodded. "Different surroundings, maybe help us forget all the shit that happened here."

"I read ya loud and clear," the sheriff said.

Roy gazed out over the highway, knowing Adriana's wounds had closed, but they would open up again if the Shadow Man ever found her. Her grandmother had died to save her, but in turn had left a curse in the young woman's blood, one traceable by evil like *Hombre Sombra*. She was a key to open a doorway to Hell, and that's why Adriana and Roy had decided to become nomads and call the highway their home. It was the only way to be certain they were never still long enough to be found.

A car parked along the curb and a woman crawled out, cussing the driver as she made her way up the sidewalk. It reminded Roy of Wanda the night she asked for his Ouija board. It also brought to mind the way she once drunkenly described the highway to him, and it gave him chills. She said life was like a highway; it ran along without stopping, through bright times and complete darkness. Each driver on it got to choose which of the million roads to take, some taking them up to heaven, while others led them straight to hell.

He hoped his highway with Adriana beside him was more like the first Wanda described, but if it turned out more like the other road, he had a crucifix and a box of bullets bathed in holy water in his glove box.

They would be ready.

# ABOUT THE AUTHORS

Dubbed the Sisters of Slaughter for their brand of horror and dark fantasy writing, Michelle Garza and Melissa Lason are a twin-sister writing team from Arizona. Their work has been published by Thunderstorm Books, Death's Head Press, and Crossroad Press. Their debut novel, *Mayan Blue*, was nominated for a Bram Stoker Award, and their short stories have been featured in many anthologies.

CPSIA information can be obtained
at www.ICGtesting.com
Printed in the USA
BVHW080855090622
639340BV00007B/186